THE FINAL SoLUTIoN

Fourth Estate
An Imprint of HarperCollins*Publishers*

THE
FINAL
SoLUTIoN

A Story of Detection

Michael Chabon

First published in a slightly different form in *The Paris Review* in 2003.

The steadfast generosity of Sir Arthur Conan Doyle enabled
the author to begin this novella; that of the MacDowell Colony
enabled him to complete it.

HarperCollins books may be purchased for educational, business, or
sales promotional use. For information, please write:
Special Markets Department, HarperCollins Publishers Inc.,
10 East 53rd Street, New York, NY 10022.

The epigraph is taken from "Alternating Currents," in
A Kiss in Space: Poems by Mary Jo Salter. Knopf, 1999.

FIRST U.S. EDITION

Printed on acid-free paper

Book design by Jennifer Ann Daddio
Illustrations by Jay Ryan

Library of Congress Cataloging-in-Publication Data
is available upon request.

ISBN 0-06-076340-X

To the memory of

AMaNDA DaVIS

first reader of these pages

The distinction's always fine
between detection and invention.

—MARY JO SALTER

THE FINAL SoLUTIoN

1

A boy with a parrot on his shoulder was walking along the railway tracks. His gait was dreamy and he swung a daisy as he went. With each step the boy dragged his toes in the rail bed, as if measuring out his journey with careful ruled marks of his shoetops in the gravel. It was midsummer, and there was something about the black hair and pale face of the boy against the green unfurling flag of the downs beyond, the rolling white eye of the daisy, the knobby knees in their short pants, the self-important air of the handsome gray parrot with its savage red tail feather, that charmed the old man as he watched them go by. Charmed him, or aroused his sense—a faculty at one time renowned throughout Europe—of promising anomaly.

The old man lowered the latest number of *The British*

Bee Journal to the rug of Shetland wool that was spread across his own knobby but far from charming knees, and brought the long bones of his face closer to the windowpane. The tracks—a spur of the Brighton-Eastbourne line, electrified in the late twenties with the consolidation of the Southern Railway routes—ran along an embankment a hundred yards to the north of the cottage, between the concrete posts of a wire fence. It was ancient glass the old man peered through, rich with ripples and bubbles that twisted and toyed with the world outside. Yet even through this distorting pane it seemed to the old man that he had never before glimpsed two beings more intimate in their parsimonious sharing of a sunny summer afternoon than these.

He was struck, as well, by their apparent silence. It seemed probable to him that in any given grouping of an African gray parrot—a notoriously prolix species—and a boy of nine or ten, at any given moment, one or the other of them ought to be talking. Here was another anomaly. As for what it promised, this the old man—though he had once made his fortune and his reputation through a long and brilliant series of extrapolations from unlikely groupings of facts—could not, could never, have begun to foretell.

As he came nearly in line with the old man's window, some one hundred yards away, the boy stopped. He turned his narrow back to the old man as if he could feel the latter's gaze upon him. The parrot glanced first to the east, then to the west, with a strangely furtive air. The boy was up to something. A hunching of the shoulders, an anticipatory flexing of the knees. It was some mysterious business—distant in time but deeply familiar—yes—

—the toothless clockwork engaged; the unstrung Steinway sounded: *the conductor rail.*

Even on a sultry afternoon like this one, when cold and damp did not trouble the hinges of his skeleton, it could be a lengthy undertaking, done properly, to rise from his chair, negotiate the shifting piles of ancient-bachelor clutter—newspapers both cheap and of quality, trousers, bottles of salve and liver pills, learned annals and quarterlies, plates of crumbs—that made treacherous the crossing of his parlor, and open his front door to the world. Indeed the daunting prospect of the journey from armchair to doorstep was among the reasons for his lack of commerce with the world, on the rare occasions when the world, gingerly taking hold of the brass door-knocker wrought in the hostile form of a giant *Apis dorsata,* came calling. Nine visitors out of ten he would sit, listening to the bemused mutterings and fumblings at the door, reminding himself that there were few now living for whom he would willingly risk catching the toe of his slipper in the hearth rug and spilling the scant remainder of his life across the cold stone floor. But as the boy with the parrot on his shoulder prepared to link his own modest puddle of electrons to the torrent of them being pumped along the conductor, or third, rail from the Southern Railway power plant on the Ouse outside of Lewes, the

old man hoisted himself from his chair with such unaccustomed alacrity that the bones of his left hip produced a disturbing scrape. Lap rug and journal slid to the floor.

He wavered a moment, groping already for the door
latch, though he still had to cross the entire room to reach it.
His failing arterial system labored to supply his suddenly
skybound brain with useful blood. His ears rang and his
knees ached and his feet were plagued with stinging. He
lurched, with a haste that struck him as positively giddy,
toward the door, and jerked it open, somehow injuring, as he
did so, the nail of his right forefinger.

"You, boy!" he called, and even to his own ears his voice
sounded querulous, wheezy, even a touch demented. "Stop
that at once!"

The boy turned. With one hand he clutched at the fly of
his trousers. With the other he cast aside the daisy. The parrot sidestepped across the boy's shoulders to the back of his
head, as if taking shelter there.

"Why, do you imagine, is there a *fence*?" the old man
said, aware that the barrier fences had not been maintained
since the war began and were in poor condition for ten miles
in either direction. "For pity's sake, you'd be fried like a
smelt!" As he hobbled across his dooryard toward the boy
on the tracks, he took no note of the savage pounding of his
heart. Or rather he noted it with anxiety and then covered
the anxiety with a hard remark. "One can only imagine the
stench."

Flower discarded, valuables restored with a zip to their lodging, the boy stood motionless. He held out to the old man a face as wan and empty as the bottom of a beggar's tin cup. The old man could hear the flatted chiming of milk cans at Satterlee's farm a quarter mile off, the agitated rustle of the housemartins under his own eaves, and, as always, the ceaseless machination of the hives. The boy shifted from one foot to the other, as if searching for an appropriate response. He opened his mouth, and closed it again. It was the parrot who finally spoke.

"*Zwei eins sieben fünf vier sieben drei,*" the parrot said, in a soft, oddly breathy voice, with the slightest hint of a lisp. The boy stood, as if listening to the parrot's statement, though his expression did not deepen or complicate. "*Vier acht vier neun eins eins sieben.*"

The old man blinked. The German numbers were so unexpected, literally so outlandish, that for a moment they registered only as a series of uncanny noises, savage avian utterances devoid of any sense.

"*Bist du deutscher?*" the old man finally managed, a little uncertain, for a moment, of whether he was addressing the boy or the parrot. It had been thirty years since he had last spoken German, and he felt the words tumble from a high back shelf of his mind.

Cautiously, with a first flicker of emotion in his gaze, the boy nodded.

The old man stuck his injured finger into his mouth and

sucked it without quite realizing that he did so, without remarking the salt flavor of his own blood. To encounter a solitary German, on the South Downs, in July 1944, and a German boy at that—here was a puzzle to kindle old appetites and energies. He felt pleased with himself for having roused his bent frame from the insidious grip of his armchair.

"How did you get here?" the old man said. "Where are you going? Where in heaven's name did you get that parrot?" Then he offered translations into German, of varying quality, for each of his questions.

The boy stood, faintly smiling as he scratched at the back of the parrot's head with two grimy fingers. The density of his silence suggested something more than unwillingness to speak; the old man wondered if the boy might be rather less German than mentally defective, incapable of sound or sense. An idea came to the old man. He held up a hand to the boy, signaling that he ought to wait just where he was. Then he withdrew once more to the gloom of his cottage. In a corner cabinet, behind a battered coal scuttle in which he had once kept his pipes, he found a dust-furred tin of violet pastilles, stamped with the portrait of a British general whose great victory had long since lost any relevance to the present situation of the Empire. The old man's retinae swam with blots and paisley tadpoles of remembered summer light, and the luminous inverted ghost of a boy with a parrot on his shoulder. He had

a sudden understanding of himself, from the boy's point of view, as a kind of irascible ogre, appearing from the darkness of his thatched cottage like something out of the Brothers Grimm, with a rusted tin of suspect sweets in his clawlike, bony hand. He was surprised, and relieved as well, to find the boy still standing there when he re-emerged.

"Here," he said, holding out the tin. "It has been many years, but in my time sweets were widely acknowledged to be a kind of juvenile Esperanto." He grinned, doubtless a crooked and ogreish grin. "Come. Have a pastille? There. Good lad."

The boy nodded, and crossed the sandy dooryard to take the confectionery from the tin. He helped himself to three or four of the little pilules, then gave a solemn nod of thanks. A mute, then; something wrong with his vocal apparatus.

"*Bitte,*" said the old man. For the first time in a very many years, he felt the old vexation, the mingled impatience and pleasure at the world's beautiful refusal to yield up its mysteries without a fight. "Now," he went on, licking his dry lips with patent ogreishness. "Tell me how you came to be so very far from home."

The pastilles rattled like beads against the boy's little teeth. The parrot worked its graphite blue beak fondly through his hair. The boy sighed, an apologetic shrug taking momentary hold of his shoulders. Then he turned and went back the way he had come.

"*Neun neun drei acht zwei sechs sieben,*" said the parrot, as they walked off into the wavering green vastness of the afternoon.

2

There were so many queer aspects to Sunday dinner at the Panicker table that Mr. Shane, the new arrival, aroused the suspicions of his fellow lodger Mr. Parkins merely by seeming to take no notice of any of them. He strode into the dining room, a grand, rubicund fellow who set the floorboards to creaking mightily when he trod them and who looked as if he keenly felt the lack of a pony between his legs. He wore his penny-red hair cropped close to the scalp and there was something indefinitely colonial, a nasal echo of cantonment or goldfields, in his speech. He nodded in turn to Parkins, to the refugee child, and to Reggie Panicker, and then flung himself into his chair like a boy settling onto the back of a school chum for a ride across the lawn. Immediately he struck up a conversation with the elder Panicker on the subject of American roses, a subject about which, he freely admitted, he knew nothing.

A profound reservoir of poise, or a pathological deficit of curiosity, Parkins supposed, might explain the near-total lack of interest that Mr. Shane, who gave himself out to be a traveler in milking equipment for the firm of Chedbourne & Jones, Yorkshire, appeared to take in the nature of his interlocutor, Mr. Panicker, who was not only a Malayalee from Kerala, black as a bootheel, but also a high-church Anglican vicar. Politesse or stupidity, perhaps, might also prevent him from remarking on the sullen way in which Reggie Panicker, the vicar's grown son, was gouging a deep hole in the tatted tablecloth with the point of his fish knife, as well as on the presence at the table of a mute nine-year-old boy whose face was like a blank back page from the book of human sorrows. But it was the way in which Mr. Shane paid so little attention to the boy's parrot that made it impossible for Mr. Parkins to accept the new lodger at face value. No one could be immune to the interest that inhered in the parrot, even if, as now, the bird was merely reciting bits and scraps of poems of Goethe and Schiller known to every German schoolchild over the age of seven. Mr. Parkins, who had, for reasons of his own, long kept the African gray under careful observation, immediately saw in the new lodger a potential rival in his ongoing quest to solve the deepest and most vexing mystery of the remarkable African bird. Clearly, Someone Important had heard about the numbers, and had sent Mr. Shane to hear them for himself.

"Well, here we are." Into the dining room swung Mrs. Panicker, carrying a Spode tureen. She was a large, plain, flaxen-haired Oxfordshirewoman whose unimaginably wild inspiration of thirty years past, to marry her father's coal-eyed, serious young assistant minister from India, had borne fruit far mealier than the ripe rosy pawpaws that she had, breathing in the scent of Mr. K. T. Panicker's hair oil on a warm summer evening in 1913, permitted herself to antici-pate. But she kept an excellent table, one that merited the custom of a far greater number of lodgers than the Panicker household currently enjoyed. The living was a minor one, the black vicar locally unpopular, the parishioners stingy as flints, and the Panicker family, in spite of Mrs. Panicker's thrift and stern providence, uncomfortably poor. It was only Mrs. Panicker's lavishly tended kitchen garden and culinary knack that could make possible a fine cold cucumber and chervil soup such as the one that she now proposed, lifting the lid of the tureen, to Mr. Shane, for whose sudden pres-ence in the house, with two months paid in advance, she was clearly grateful.

"Now, I'm warning you well beforehand, this time, Master Steinman," she said as she ladled pale green cream, flecked with emerald, into the boy's bowl, "it's a *cold* soup and meant to be." She looked at Mr. Shane, frowning, though her eyes held a faint glint of amusement. "Sprayed the whole table with cream soup, last week, did the boy, Mr. Shane," she went on. "Ruined Reggie's best cravat."

"If only that were the most this boy had ruined," Reggie said, from behind his spoonful of cucumber soup. "If only we could leave it at a cravat."

Reggie Panicker was the despair of the Panickers and, like many sons who betray even the most modest aspirations of their parents, a scourge of the neighborhood as well. He was a gambler, a liar, a malcontent, and a sneak. Parkins—showing, it now seemed to him, a certain thickness of wit—had lost a pair of gold cufflinks, a box of pen nibs, twelve shillings, and his good luck charm, a blond five-franc chip from the Casino Royale in Monaco, before catching on to Reggie's thieving ways.

"And how old would young Mr. Steinman be, then?" Mr. Shane said, training the flashing heliograph of his smile on the faraway eyes of the little Jew. "Nine is it? Are you nine, boy?"

As usual, though, the lookouts in the head of Linus Steinman had been left unmanned. The smile went unacknowledged. The boy seemed, in fact, not to have heard the question, though Parkins had long since established that there was nothing wrong with his ears. The sudden clatter of a plate could make him jump. The tolling of the bell in the church tower could fill his great dark eyes with unaccountable tears.

"You won't get answers out of that one," Reggie said, tipping the last of his soup into his mouth. "Dumb as a mallet, is that one."

The boy looked down at his soup. He frowned. He was regarded by most of the residents of the vicarage, and in the neighborhood, as non-Anglophonic and quite possibly stupid. But Parkins had his doubts on both scores.

"Master Steinman came to us from Germany," Mr. Panicker said. He was a learned man whose Oxford accent was tinged with a disappointed subcontinental lilt. "He formed part of a small group of children, most of them Jewish, whose emigration to Britain was negotiated by Mr. Wilkes, the vicar of the English Church in Berlin."

Shane nodded, mouth open, eyes blinking slowly, like a golfing man pretending to enjoy for courtesy's sake an impromptu lecture on cell mitosis or irrational numbers. He might never have heard of Germany or Jews or, for that matter, of vicars or children. The air of deep boredom that settled over his features looked entirely natural to them. And yet Mr. Parkins mistrusted it. The parrot, whose name was Bruno, was now reciting from *Der Erlkönig*, softly, even one might have said politely, in its high, halting voice. The bird's delivery, though toneless and a bit rushed, had a childish poignancy not inappropriate to the subject of the poem. And yet still the new lodger had taken no notice of the parrot.

Mr. Shane looked at the boy, who looked down at his

soup, dipping the merest tip of his spoon into the thick pale bowlful. As far as Parkins had ever observed—and he was a careful and pointed observer—the boy ate with relish only sweets and puddings.

"Nazis, was it?" said Shane. He gave his head a moderate shake. "Rotten business. Tough luck for the Jews, when you come right down to it." The question of whether or not the boy was going to spit out the bit of soup he had dabbed onto his tongue appeared to interest him far more than had the internment of the Jews. The boy frowned, and knit his thick eyebrows together. But the soup remained safely in his mouth, and at last Mr. Shane turned his attention to polishing off his own portion. Parkins wondered if the dull and unpleasant subject were now to be dropped.

"No place for a child, to be sure," said Shane. "A camp of that sort. Nor, I imagine—" He laid down his spoon and raised his eyes, with a swiftness that startled Mr. Parkins, to the corner of the room where, on top of a heavy iron pole, on a scarred wooden crosspiece, with pages of yesterday's *Express* spread underneath, Bruno the parrot gazed critically back at him. "—for a parrot."

Ah, thought Mr. Parkins.

"I suppose you think a wretched stone hovel in the dullest corner of Sussex is a fine place for an African bird, then," Reggie Panicker said.

Mr. Shane blinked.

"Please excuse my son's rudeness," Mr. Panicker said, with a sigh, laying down his own spoon though his bowl was only half empty. If there had been a time when he reprimanded the steady churlishness of his only child, it predated Mr. Parkins's tenure in the house. "We have all grown very fond of young Linus and his pet, as it happens. And really, Bruno is a most remarkable animal. He recites poetry, as you hear now. He sings songs. He is a most gifted mimic and has already startled my wife a number of times by counterfeiting my own, perhaps overly vehement, manner of sneezing."

"Really?" Mr. Shane said. "Well, Mr. Panicker, I hope you won't mind my saying that between your roses and this young chap with his parrot, I seem to have landed myself in a very interesting household."

He was watching the bird, head cocked to one side in a way that echoed, no doubt unconsciously, the angle from which Bruno habitually preferred to view the world.

"Sings does he?"

"That's right. Principally in German, though from time to time one hears snatches of Gilbert & Sullivan. Chiefly bits of *Iolanthe*, as far as I can tell. Quite startling the first few times."

"But is it all rote—*parroting*, as it were?" Mr. Shane smiled thinly, as if to imply, insincerely Mr. Parkins thought, that he knew his little joke was not amusing. "Or is he capable of actual thought, would you say? I once saw a pig, as a boy, a performing pig, that could find the square root of three-digit numbers."

His gaze, as he said this, flashed briefly and for the first time toward Parkins. This, though it seemed to confirm Mr. Parkins's hunch about the new lodger, also troubled him. As far as anyone in the neighborhood knew, there was no reason to connect him with the subject of digits and numbers. The suspicion that Mr. Shane had been sent by Certain People to observe Bruno firsthand, Mr. Parkins now considered to have been confirmed.

"Numbers," Mr. Panicker said. "Oddly enough, Bruno seems quite fond of them, doesn't he, Mr. Parkins? Always rattling off great chains and lists of them. All in German, naturally. Though I can't say that he appears to do anything with them that I'm aware of."

"No? He keeps me from sleeping," Reggie said. "That's use enough for me. That's *startling* enough for me, all right."

At this point Mrs. Panicker swept back into the dining room carrying the fish course on a pale green platter. For reasons that had never been articulated to Mr. Parkins but which he felt must have a good deal to do with her otherwise unexpressed feelings about her husband and son, she never joined them for dinner. She cleared away the bowls as Mr. Parkins muttered his approval of the soup. There was something desperate and brave about the landlady's good cookery. It was like the quavering voice of a bagpipe, issuing forth from a citadel that was invested on all sides by dervishes and infidels on the morning of the day on which it would finally be sacked.

"Excellent soup!" barked Mr. Shane. "Compliments to the chef!"

Mrs. Panicker flushed deeply, and a smile unlike any that Parkins had ever seen there, tiny and pouting, made a brief appearance on her lips.

Mr. Panicker noticed it too, and frowned.

"Indeed," he said.

"Phew!" said the younger Panicker, fanning away the steam that rose from the platter on which lay a plaice that retained its head and tail. "That fish is off, Mother. It smells like the underside of Brighton Pier."

Without missing a beat—with a last trace of the girlish smile still lingering—Mrs. Panicker reached across and slapped Reggie's face. Her son leapt from his seat, a hand to his blazing cheek, and for a moment he only glared at her. Then his hand shot out toward her throat as if he meant to choke her. Before his fingers could find purchase, however, the new lodger was on his feet and had interposed himself between mother and son. Mr. Shane's hands flew out in front of him and before Parkins quite understood what was happening Reggie Panicker was lying flat on his back on the oval rug. Bright blood sprang from his nose.

He sat up. Blood dripped onto his collar and he dabbed at it with a finger, then pressed the finger against his left nostril. Mr. Shane offered him a hand, and Reggie batted it aside. He got to his feet and snuffled deeply. He stared at Shane, then nodded toward Mrs. Panicker.

"Mother," he said. Then he turned and went out.

"Mother," said the parrot, in his soft voice. Linus Steinman was looking at Bruno with the deep affection that was the only recognizable emotion Parkins had ever seen the boy express. And then, in a clear, fluting, tender voice Parkins had never heard, the bird began to sing.

Wien, Wien, Wien
Sterbende Märchenstadt

It was a lovely contralto and, as it issued jerkily from the bill of the gray animal in the corner, disturbingly human. They listened for a moment, and then Linus Steinman rose from his chair and went to the perch. The bird fell silent, and stepped onto the outstretched forearm that was proffered. The boy turned back to them, and his eyes were filled with tears and with a simple question as well.

"Yes, dear," said Mrs. Panicker with a sigh. "You may as well be excused."

3

They found him sitting on the boot bench outside his front door, hatted and caped in spite of the heat, sunburnt hands clasping the head of his blackthorn stick. All ready to go. As if—though it was impossible—he were expecting them. They must have caught him on his doorstep, boots laced, gathering his strength for a late-morning tramp across the Downs.

"Which one are you?" he said to Inspector Bellows. His eye was exceedingly bright. The great beak quivered as if catching scent of them. "Speak up."

"Bellows," said the inspector. "Detective Inspector Michael Bellows. Sorry to bother you, sir. But I am new on the job, down here, learning the ropes, as they say, and I don't at all overrate my capacities."

At this last assertion the inspector's companion, Detective

Constable Quint, cleared his throat and politely directed his gaze toward the middle distance.

"Bellows . . . I knew your father," the old man suggested. Head tottering on his feeble neck. Cheeks flecked with the blood and plaster of an old man's hasty shave. "Surely? In the West End. Red-haired chap, ginger mustache. Specialized, as I recall, in confidence men. Not without ability I should have said."

"Sandy Bellows," the inspector said. "*Grand*father, actually. And how often did I hear him speak highly of you, sir."

Not quite so often, perhaps, the inspector thought, as I heard him curse your name.

The old man nodded, gravely. The inspector's sharp eye detected a fleeting sadness, a flicker of memory that briefly seamed the old man's face.

"I have known a great many policemen," he said. "A great many." He brightened, willfully. "But it is always a pleasure to make the acquaintance of another. And Detective Constable . . . *Quint*, I believe?"

He trained his raptor gaze now on the constable, a dark, brooding potato-nosed fellow. DC Quint was much attached, as he rarely neglected to let it be known, to the prior detective inspector, sadly deceased but a proponent apparently of the old solid methods of policework. Quint tipped a finger to the brim of his hat. Not a talkative fellow, DC Quint.

"Now, who has died, and by what means?" the old man said.

"A man named Shane, sir. Struck in the back of the head with a blunt object."

The old man looked unimpressed. Even, perhaps, disappointed.

"Ah," he said. "Shane struck in the back of the head. Blunt object. I see."

Perhaps a bit batty after all, thought the inspector. *Not what he used to be,* as Quint had put it. *Pity.*

"I am not in the least senile, Inspector, I assure you," the old man said. He had read the trend of the inspector's thoughts; no, that was impossible, too. Read his *face,* then; the cant of his shoulders. "But this is a crucial moment, a crisis, if you will, in the hives. I could not possibly abandon them for an unremarkable crime."

Bellows glanced at his constable. The inspector was young enough, and murder rare enough on the South Downs, for it to seem to both policemen that there was perhaps *something* remarkable about a man's skull being staved in with a poker or a sap, behind a vicarage.

"And this Shane was armed, sir," DC Quint said. "Carried a Webley service pistol, for all that he claimed to be, and near as we can tell he *were,* nothing but a commercial traveler in—" He pulled a small oilskin-covered notepad from his pocket and consulted it. The inspector had already learned to detest the sight of that notepad with its careful inventory of deeply irrelevant facts. "—the dairy machine and equipment line."

"Hit from behind," the inspector said. "It appears. In the dead of night as he was about to get into his motor. Bags all packed, apparently leaving town with no explanation or goodbye, though only just a week before he prepaid two months' lodging at the vicarage."

"The vicarage, yes, I see." The old man closed his eyes, heavily, as if the facts in the case were not merely unremarkable but soporific. "And no doubt you have, quite literally *unadvisedly,* since you can have received no sensible counsel in the matter, leapt to the readiest conclusion, and placed young Mr. *Panicker* under arrest for the crime."

Though aware of the silent film comedy aspect of their behavior, Inspector Bellows found to his shame he couldn't prevent himself from exchanging another sheep-faced look with his constable. Reggie Panicker had been arrested at ten that morning, three hours after the discovery of the body of Richard Woolsey Shane, of Sevenoaks, Kent, in the lane behind the vicarage where the deceased had parked his 1933 MG Midget.

"For which crime," continued the old man, "that lamentable young man in the fullness of time will duly be hanged by the neck, and his mother will weep, and then the world will continue to roll blindly on its way through the void, and in the end your Mr. Shane will still be dead. But in the meantime, Inspector, *Number 4 must be re-queened.*"

And he waved a long-fingered starfish hand, all warts

and speckles, dismissing them. Sending them along their way. He patted down the pockets of his wrinkled suit: looking for his pipe.

"A parrot is missing!" Inspector Michael Bellows tried, helpless, hoping this titbit might in the old man's unimaginable estimation add some kind of luster to the crime. "And we found this on the person of the vicar's son."

He drew from his breast pocket the dog-eared calling card of Mr. Jos. Black, Dealer in Rare and Exotic Birds, Club Row, London, and submitted it to the old man, who did not give it a glance.

"A *parrot.*" Somehow, Bellows saw, he had managed not merely to impress but to astonish the old man. And the old man looked delighted to so find himself. "Yes, of course. An African gray. Belonging, perhaps, to a small boy. Aged about nine years. A German national—of Jewish origin, I'd wager—and incapable of speech."

Now would have been the moment for the inspector to clear his own throat. DC Quint had argued strenuously against involving the old man in the investigation. *He's strictly non compos sir, I can heartily assure you of that.* But Inspector Bellows was too flummoxed to gloat. He had heard the tales, the legends, the wild, famous leaps of induction pulled off by the old man in his heyday, assassins inferred from cigar ash, horse thieves from the absence of a watchdog's bark. Try as he might, the inspector could not find the way to a mute German jewboy from a missing parrot and a corpse named Shane with a ventilated skull. And so he missed his opportunity to score a point off DC Quint.

Now the old man had a look at Mr. Jos. Black's calling card, lips pursed, dragging it across a range of distances from the tip of his nose until he settled on one that would do.

"Ah," he said, nodding. "So our Mr. Shane came upon young Panicker as he was making off with the poor boy's pet, which he hoped to sell to this Mr. Black. And Shane attempted to prevent him from doing so, and so paid dearly for his heroism. Do I fairly summarize your view?"

Though this was in short the whole of his theory, from the first there had been something in it—something in the circumstances of the murder itself—that troubled the inspector enough to send him, against the advice of his constable, calling on this half-legendary friend and adversary of his grandfather's entire generation of policemen. Nevertheless it had sounded a sensible enough theory, all in all. The old man's tone, however, rendered it as likely as the agency of fairies.

"Apparently there were words between them," the inspector said, wincing as an ancient stammer resurfaced from the depths of his boyhood. "They quarreled. It came to blows."

"Yes, yes. Well, I don't doubt that you are right."

The old man composed the seam of his mouth into the most insincere smile Inspector Bellows had ever seen.

"And, really," he continued, "it is most fortunate that you require so little assistance from me, since, as you must know, I am retired. As indeed I have been since the tenth of August, 1914. At which time, you may take it from me, I was far less sunk in decrepitude than the withered carapace you now see before you." He tapped the shaft of his stick juridically against the doorstep. They were dismissed. "Good day."

And then, with an echo of the love of theatrics that had so tried the patience and enlivened the language of the inspector's grandfather, the old man tilted his face up to the sun, and closed his eyes.

The two policemen stood a moment, watching this shameless simulacrum of an afternoon nap. It crossed the inspector's mind that perhaps the old man wished them to plead with him. He glanced at DC Quint. No doubt abject pleading with the mad old hermit was a step to which his late predecessor would never have been reduced. And yet how much there was to be learned from such a man if only one could—

The eyes snapped open, and now the smile hardened into something more sincere and cruel.

"Still here?" he said.

"Sir—if I may—"

"Very well." The old man chuckled dryly, entirely to himself. "I have considered the needs of my bees. And I believe that I can spare a few hours. Therefore I will assist you." He held up a long, admonishing finger. *"To find the boy's parrot."* Laboriously, and with an air that rebuffed in advance any offers of assistance, the old man, relying heavily on his scarred black stick, hoisted himself onto his feet. "If we should encounter the actual murderer along the way, well, then it will be so much the better for you."

4

The old man settled himself onto one knee. The left one; the right knee was no good for anything anymore. It took him a damnably long time, and on the way down there was a horrible snapping sound. But he managed it and went about his work with dispatch. He pulled off his right glove and poked his naked finger into the bloody mud where Richard Woolsey Shane's life had seeped away. Then he reached into the old conjuror's pocket sewn into the lining of his cloak and took out his glass. It was brass and tortoise shell, and bore around its bezel an affectionate inscription from the sole great friend of his life.

With a series of huffings and grunts, laboring across twenty feet square of level ground as if they were the sheer icy face of Karakorum, the old man turned his beloved lens upon everything that occupied or surrounded the fatal spot, tucked between the lush green hedgerows of Hallows Lane, at which Shane's half-headless body had been found, early that morning, by his landlord, Mr. Panicker. Alas that the body had already been moved, and by clumsy men in heavy boots! All that remained was its faint imprint, a twisted cross in the dust. On the right tire of the dead man's motorcar—awfully flash for a traveler in milking machines—he noted the centripetal pattern and moderate degree of darkening in the feathery spray of blood on the tire's white wall. Though the police had made a search of the car, turning up an ordnance survey map of Sussex, a length of clear rubber milking hose, bits of valve and pipe, several glossy prospectuses for the Chedbourne & Jones Lactrola R-5, and a well-thumbed copy of Treadley's *Common Diseases of Milch Kine*, 1926 edition, the old man went over the whole thing again. All the while, though he was unaware of it, he kept up a steady muttering, nodding his head from time to time, carrying on one half of a conversation, and showing a certain impatience with his invisible interlocutor. This procedure required nearly forty minutes, but when he emerged from the car, feeling quite as if he ought to lie down, he was holding a live .45 caliber cartridge for that highly unlikely Webley, and an unsmoked Murat cigarette, an Egyptian brand whose choice by the victim, were it his, seemed to indicate still greater unsuspected depths of experience or romance. Finally he dug around in the mulchy earth that lay beneath the hedgerows, finding in the process a piece of shattered cranium, stuck with bits of skin and hair, that the policemen, to their evident discomfiture, had missed.

He handled the grisly bit of evidence without hesitation or qualm. He had seen human beings in every state, phase, and attitude of death: a Cheapside drab tumbled, throat cut, headfirst down a stairway of the Thames Embankment, blood pooling in her mouth and eye sockets; a stolen child, green as a kelpie, stuffed into a storm drain; the papery pale husk of a pensioner, killed with arsenic over the course of a dozen years; a skeleton looted by kites and dogs and countless insects, bleached and creaking in a wood, tattered garments fluttering like flags; a pocketful of teeth and bone chips in a shovelful of pale incriminating ash. There was nothing remarkable, nothing at all, about the crooked X that death had scrawled in the dust of Hallows Lane.

At last he put the glass away and stood up as straight as he could manage. He gave a last look around at the situation of the hedgerows, the MG under its tarpaulin of dust, the behavior of the rooks, the direction taken by the coal smoke streaming from the chimney of the vicarage. Then he turned to the young inspector, studying him at some length without speaking.

"Anything wrong?" Sandy Bellows's grandson said. So far the old man had refrained from asking the inspector whether his grandfather was living or dead. He knew all too well what the answer would be.

"You have done a fine job," the old man said. "First rate."

The inspector smiled, and his eyes traveled to the sullen Constable Quint, standing by the little green roadster. The constable pulled on one half of his mustache and glowered at the muddy purple puddle at his feet.

"Shane *was* approached and struck, with considerable force, from behind; you have that much right. Tell me, Inspector, how you square that with your idea that the deceased came upon and surprised young Mr. Panicker in the act of stealing the parrot?"

Bellows started to speak, then left off with a short, weary sigh, and shook his head. DC Quint tugged his mustache down now, in an attempt to conceal the smile that had formed on his lips.

"The pattern and frequency of footprints indicates," the old man continued, "that at the moment the blow fell Mr. Shane was moving in some haste, and carrying something in his left hand, something rather heavy, I should wager. Since your men found his valise and all of his personal effects by the garden door, as if waiting to be transferred to the boot of the car, and since the birdcage is nowhere to be found, I think it reasonable to infer that Shane was fleeing, when he was murdered, *with* the birdcage. Presumably the bird was in it, though I think a thorough search of neighborhood trees ought to be made, and soon."

The young inspector turned to DC Quint and nodded once. DC Quint let go of his mustache. He looked aghast.

"You can't mean, sir, with all due respect, that you want *me* to waste valuable time staring up into trees looking for a—"

"Oh, you needn't worry, Detective Constable," the old man said, with a wink. He did not care to divulge his hypothesis—naturally only one of several under consideration—that Bruno the African gray parrot might be clever enough to have engineered an escape from his captor. Men, policemen in particular, tended to discount the capacity of animals to enact, often with considerable panache, the foulest of crimes and the most daring stunts. "You can't miss the tail."

Constable Quint seemed unable for a moment to gain control of the musculature of his jaw. Then he turned and stomped off down the lane, toward the trellised doorway that led into the garden of the vicarage.

"As for you." The old man turned to the inspector. "You must seek to inform yourself about our victim. I will want to see the body, of course. I suspect we may discover—"

A woman screamed, grandly at first, almost one would have said with a hint of melody. Then her cry disintegrated into a series of little gasping barks:

Oh oh oh oh oh—

The inspector took off at a run, leaving the old man to follow scraping and hobbling along behind. When he came into the garden he saw a number of familiar objects and entities set about on an expanse of green as if arranged to a de-

sired effect or inferable purpose, like counters or chessmen in some kingly recreation. Regarding them the old man experienced a moment of vertiginous horror during which he could neither reckon their number nor recall their names or purposes. He felt—with all his body, as one felt the force of gravity or inertia—the inevitability of his failure. The conquest of his mind by age was not a mere blunting or slowing down but an erasure, as of a desert capital by a drifting millennium of sand. Time had bleached away the ornate pattern of his intellect, leaving a blank white scrap. He feared then that he was going to be sick, and raised the head of his stick to his mouth. It was cold against his lips. The horror seemed to subside at once; consciousness rallied itself around the brutal taste of metal, and all at once he found himself looking, with inexpressible relief, merely at the two policemen, Bellows and Quint; at Mr. and Mrs. Panicker, standing on either side of a birdbath; at a handsome Jew in a black suit; a sundial; a wooden chair; a hawthorn bush in lavish flower. They were all gazing upward to the peak of the vicarage's thatched roof at the remaining token in the game.

"Young man, you will come down from there at once!"

The voice was that of Mr. Panicker—who was rather more intelligent than the average country parson, in the old man's view, and rather less competent to minister to the souls of his parishioners. He backed a step or two away from the house as if to find a better spot from which to fix the boy on the roof of the house with a baleful stare. But the vicar's eyes were far too large and sorrowful, the old man thought, ever to do the trick.

"Sonny boy," Constable Quint called up. "You're going to break your neck!"

The boy stood, upright, hands dangling by his sides, feet together, teetering on the fulcrum of his heels. He looked neither distressed nor playful, merely gazed down at his shoes or at the ground far below him. The old man wondered if he could have gone up there to search for his parrot. Perhaps in the past the bird had been known to take refuge on housetops.

"Fetch a ladder," the inspector said.

The boy slipped, and went sliding on his bottom down the long thatch slope of the roof toward the edge. Mrs. Panicker let out another scream. At the last moment the boy gripped two fistfuls of thatch and held on to them. His progress was arrested with a jerk, and then the handfuls ripped free of the roof and he sailed out into the void and plummeted to earth, landing on top of the good-looking young Jewish man, a Londoner by the cut of his suit, with a startling crunch like a barrel shattering against rocks. After a dazed moment the boy stood up, and shook his hands as if they stung him. Then he offered one to the man on his belly on the ground.

"Mr. Kalb," cried Mrs. Panicker, scurrying over, a hand

pressed to the necklace at her bosom, to the side of the dapper Londoner. "Good heavens, are you hurt?"

Mr. Kalb accepted the hand the child offered him, and pretended to let the boy drag him to his feet. Though he winced and groaned, the grin did not leave his face for a moment.

"Not terribly. A bruised rib perhaps. It's nothing at all."

He held out his hands to the boy, and the boy stepped between them. Mr. Kalb, with a visible wince, lifted him into the air. Only once he was safely in the arms of the visitor from London, for reasons that the old man felt a powerful desire to understand, did the boy relax his grip over his emotions, and mourn, wildly and uncontrollably, the loss of his friend, burying his face in Mr. Kalb's shoulder.

The old man made his way across the garden.

"Boy," he said. "Do you remember me?"

The boy looked up, his face flushed and swollen. A delicate span of mucus connected the tip of his nose to the lapel of Mr. Kalb's jacket.

The inspector introduced the old man to the mournful-eyed man from the Aid Committee, Mr. Martin Kalb. Mrs. Panicker had sent for him as soon as Bruno went missing that morning. When he heard the old man's name, something flickered, a dim memory, in the eyes of Mr. Kalb. He smiled, and turned to the boy.

"Well," he said, in German that the old man understood a few moments after the words were spoken, giving the boy's shoulder an encouraging squeeze. "Here is the man to find your bird. Now you have nothing to worry about."

"Mrs. Panicker," the old man said, over his shoulder. The blood drained from the woman's face—every bit, though he did not suspect her for a moment, as if he had caught her without an alibi. "I shall want to speak to your son. I am sure that the police will have no objection to your coming along with a clean shirt and a packet of biscuits."

5

She packed a pair of shirts, two pairs of socks, two pairs of neatly pressed underpants. A brand-new toothbrush. A cheese, a packet of crackers, and an ancient, prerationing box of the sultanas he liked. The lot barely filled a small grip. She put on her good blue dress with the mandarin collar and then went downstairs to find the boy.

Even before the theft of Bruno, Linus had been prone to disappearance. He seemed less a boy to her than the shadow of a boy, stealing through the house, the village, the world. He had mouseholes everywhere, in shaded corners of the churchyard, under the eaves of the vicarage, in the belfry of the church tower itself. He wandered off into the countryside with the bird on his shoulder, and though she disapproved strongly of this, she had given up trying to stop him, because she could never bring herself to punish the poor child. She didn't have the heart. At any rate she had treated her Reggie with a strictness that did not come at all naturally to her, and look how he had turned out in the end.

She found him down by the stream at the foot of the churchyard. There was a mossy stone bench there on which six or seven hundred years of villagers, no doubt, had come to sit under the spreading yew tree, thinking mournful thoughts. Martin Kalb sat beside him. Linus had taken off his shoes and socks. And Mr. Kalb went barefoot too. For some reason the sight of his pale feet poking naked from the turn-ups of his fine gray pinstripe trousers shocked Mrs. Panicker.

"I am going out," she said, too loudly. She knew it was awful of her but she could not help shouting at the boy as if he were deaf. "I must pay a visit to Reggie. Mr. Kalb, I hope you will stay the night with us."

Mr. Kalb nodded. He had a long, sweet face, plain and studious. He reminded her of Mr. Panicker at the age of twenty-six. "Naturally."

"You can stay in Linus's room. There are two beds."

Mr. Kalb looked at the boy, raising an eyebrow. As if out of respect for the boy's muteness he spoke to the boy very little. The boy nodded. Mr. Kalb nodded. Mrs. Panicker felt a rush of gratitude.

The boy took his pad from his jacket, and his bit of green pencil. He painstakingly scrawled something on one page; he wrote only with great difficulty, chewing on his lower lip. For a moment he studied what he had written.

Then he showed the page to Mr. Kalb. She could never make head or tail of the things he wrote down.

"He asks if Mr. Shane is really dead," said Mr. Kalb.

"Yes," she fairly shouted, and then, more softly, "he is."

Linus stared up at her with his enormous brown eyes, and nodded, once, almost to himself. It was impossible to say what he was thinking. It nearly always was. Though she pitied him, and remembered him in her prayers, and in some strange way felt also that she loved him, there was something more deeply alien to her about Linus than his nationality or race could explain. Though he was a good-looking boy and the bird a handsome animal—and both of them surprisingly clean in their habits—there was an intensity in their attachment to each other that Mrs. Panicker found eerier than the bird's numerical tirades or its singing with a sweetness that froze the heart.

The boy wrestled a few more words out of his pencil stub. Mr. Kalb scanned, then, with a sigh, translated them.

" 'He was kind to me,' " he said.

Mrs. Panicker tried to reply, but she seemed to have lost her voice. Something elbowed its way up into her rib cage. Then to her shame and dismay she burst lavishly into tears. It was the first time that she had cried since sometime in the late twenties, though the Lord knew that she had reason enough to cry. She cried because this boy, this somehow bruised or dented boy, had lost his parrot. She cried because her son was sitting in a cell under the town hall, a prisoner of the Crown. And she cried because at the age of forty-seven, after twenty-five years of piety, disappointment, and restraint, she had taken a deeply foolish interest in the new lodger Mr. Richard Shane, like someone out of a coarse novel.

She went to the boy and stood before him. She had washed his bottom and combed his hair. She had fed him, and clothed him, and caught his vomit in a basin when he was sick. But she had never embraced him. She put out her hands; he sat forward, and laid his head, a bit carefully, against her belly. Mr. Kalb cleared his throat. She could feel the weight of his not looking at them as she patted the boy's hair and tried to gather herself together for the visit to the jail. She was embarrassed at weeping in front of the young man from the Aid Committee. After a moment she glanced at him and saw that he was proffering a handkerchief. She took it with a murmur of thanks.

The boy drew back, studying her while she dabbed at her eyes. She was absurdly touched to see how concerned he looked. He patted her hand as if he wanted her to pay particularly close inspection to what he had to say next. Then he scrawled four more words on his little pad. Mr. Kalb examined them with a frown. The boy's writing was atrocious, rudimentary. He reversed letters and even words, especially on those rare occasions when he tried to communicate in English. Once he had greatly discomfited her husband with a written query reading WHY DOG OV KRISCHIN DON'T LIKE JUDISH SDIK?

" 'Ask the old man,' " Mr. Kalb read.

"What on earth should I ask him?" said Mrs. Panicker.

Only once before had she seen the old man, in 1936, at the railway station, when he had emerged from his bee-crazed hermitage to meet five enormous crates sent down to him from London. Mrs. Panicker was bound for Lewes that morning, but when the old man shuffled onto the south-bound platform, accompanied by the strapping eldest son of his neighbor Walt Satterlee, she crossed over to get a better look at him. Years and years ago his name—itself redolent now of the fustian and rectitude of that vanished era—had adorned the newspapers and police gazettes of the empire, but it was his more recent, local celebrity, founded almost exclusively on legends of his shyness, irascibility, and hostility to all human commerce, that drew her across to his side of the platform that morning. Thin as a whippet, she had later reported to her husband, with something canine, or rather lupine, in the face as well, the heavy-lidded eyes intelligent and watchful and pale. They took in the features and furnishings of the platform, the texts of the posted notices, the discarded end of a cigar, a starling's ragged nest in the rafters of the overhanging roof. And then he had trained them, those lupine eyes, on her. The hunger in them so startled her that she took a step backward, striking her head against an iron pillar with such force that she later found crumbs of dried blood in her hair. It was a purely impersonal hunger, if such a thing there was—and here her report to Mr. Panicker faltered under the burden of his disapproval for her "romantic nature"—a hunger devoid of prurience, appetite, malice, or goodwill. It was a hunger, she decided later, for *information*. And yet there was liveliness in his gaze, a kind of cool vitality that was nearly amusement, as if a steady lifelong diet of mundane observations had preserved the youthfulness of his optic organs alone. Stooped in the manner of tall old men, but not bent, he had stood in the full April sunshine wrapped in a thick woolen Inverness, studying her, inspecting her, making no effort to conceal or dissemble his examination. The cloak, she remembered, had been heavily patched, with total disregard for pattern or stuff, and darned in a hundred places in a motley spectrum of colored thread.

Presently the train from London had pulled in, disgorging the great crates, punched with round holes at regular intervals, and stamped with the gentleman's antique name. Clearly visible on the side of each crate was the stenciled address of a city in Texas, U.S.A. Later she learned that they had contained, among other outlandish items, heavy trays packed with the eggs of a variety of honeybee hitherto unknown in Britain.

Mr. Panicker's reply, when she finished her account, had been a characteristic one.

"I am sorry to learn that our good English bees are insufficient to his purposes," he had said.

Now she was sitting beside him, in a back room of the

town hall. Through the lone window from the vacant lot beyond there radiated as if drawn by the old man himself the murmur of bees, insistent as the stifling afternoon itself. The old man had been stoking and sipping at his pipe for the last fifteen minutes as they awaited the prisoner. The smoke of his tobacco was the foulest that she, a girl raised in a house with seven brothers and a widowed father, had ever been obliged to inhale. It hung in the room as thick as sheepshearing and made arabesques in the harsh slanting light from the window.

As she watched the vines of smoke twisting in the sunlight, she tried to picture her son as he went about the business of murdering that fine, vital man. Nothing that she saw in her imaginings wholly persuaded her. Mrs. Panicker, née Ginny Stallard, had seen two men killed, on different occasions, during her girlhood. The first was Huey Blake, drowned by her brothers in Piltdown Pond during a semi-friendly bout of wrestling. The other was her father, the Reverend Oliver Stallard, shot at Sunday dinner by old Mr. Catley after he went off his head. Though all the world blamed her black husband for the unstable character of her one and only son, Mrs. Panicker suspected that the fault lay squarely with her. The Stallard men had always been blackguards or misfortunates. She was almost inclined to view the fact that it was taking Reggie so long to be brought up from the cells as yet one more example, though heaven knew none was needed, of her son's poor character. She could not imagine what was keeping him.

The sudden touch of the old man's dry fingers on the back of her right hand made her heart leap in her chest.

"Please," he said, with a glance at her fingers, and she saw that she had taken off her wedding ring and held it pinched tightly between the thumb and first. Clearly she had been tap-tapping the ring against the arm of her chair for quite some time, perhaps from the moment she sat down in the waiting room. The sound of it echoed dimly in her memory.

"I'm sorry," she said. She looked down at the spotted hand on hers. He removed it.

"I know how difficult this must be," he said, and smiled in a reassuring way that was, surprisingly, reassuring. "Mustn't despair."

"He didn't do it," she said.

"That remains to be seen," the old man said. "But so far, I confess, I am inclined to agree with you."

"I have no illusions about my son, sir."

"The hallmark of a sensible parent, no doubt."

"He took a disliking to Mr. Shane. It *is* true." She was a truthful woman. "But Reggie takes a disliking to everyone. He can't seem to help it."

Then the door opened, and they brought poor Reggie in. There was a plaster on his cheek, and an oblong welt across his left temple, and his nose looked too big, somehow, and all purple across the bridge. She experienced the false realization that these injuries had befallen him during his fatal struggle with Mr. Shane, and the fleeting hope of a claim of self-defense darted through her thoughts before she remembered having overheard Detective Constable Quint tell her husband that Shane was killed from behind, by a single blow to the head; there had been no struggle. A look at the faces of the policemen, eyes steady on the corners of the room as they handled Reggie to the empty chair, and the true realization set in.

The old man rose and jabbed the air with the stem of his pipe in the direction of her son.

"Has this man been harmed?" he said, his voice thin even to her ears, petulant, as if there were a kind of moral obviousness to the beating her son had been given by the police that trumped any craven protest he or anyone might register. The horror of it vied in her thoughts with a low rough voice whispering *Had it coming. Had it coming now a very long time.* It took all of her powers of self-possession— a considerable resource, strengthened through a lifetime of nearly continuous exercise—to refrain from crossing the room and taking his battered dark head in her arms, if only to smooth the disorder of his thick black mat of hair.

The two policemen, communicants of Mr. Panicker, Noakes and Woollett as she at last succeeded in putting names to them, stood blinking at the old man as if there were a bit of breakfast clinging to his lip.

"Had a fall," said the one she believed to be Noakes.

Woollett nodded. "Bad luck, that," he said.

"Indeed," the old man said. The expression drained from his face as he made another of his long, deep examinations, this time of the outraged face of her son, who stared back at the old man with a look of hatred that failed to astonish her, any more than she was surprised when in the end Reggie's gaze faltered, and he stared down, looking much younger than his twenty-two years, at his skinny brown wrists crossed in his lap.

"What's *she* doing here?" he said at last.

"Your mother has brought a few personal articles," the old man said. "I'm sure they will be welcome. But if you like, I will ask her to wait outside."

Reggie looked up, at her, and in his pout there was something that resembled thanks, a sardonic gratitude as if perhaps she were not quite as horrid a mother as he had always believed. Though in her own accounting—and she was not generous with herself—she had never failed him, every time she stood by him he seemed to view it with the same skeptical surprise.

"I don't give a damn what she does," he said.

"No," the old man said dryly. "No, I don't suppose you do. Now. Hah. Hmm. Yes. All right. Tell me, why don't you, about your friend Mr. Black, of Club Row."

"There's nothing to tell," Reggie said. "Don't know the bloke."

"Mr. Panicker," the old man said. "I am eighty-nine years old. The little life that remains to me I would much prefer to spend in the company of creatures far more intelligent and mysterious than you. Therefore, in the interest of conserving the scant time I have, allow *me* to tell *you* about Mr. Black of

Club Row. Word has lately reached his ear, I imagine, of a remarkable parrot, mature and in good health, with a gift for mimicry and a retentive mind far beyond the norm for its species. Were it his, our Mr. Black might sell this bird to a British or Continental fancier for a handsome sum. You had made up your mind, therefore, and got everything in readiness, to steal the bird and sell it to him, in the hopes of raising a large sum of cash. Which cash, if I am not mistaken, you require to repay the debt you have incurred to Fatty Hodges."

The words were spoken and left behind before her thoughts could catch up to them or to the instantaneous jolt they had sent straight through her. Fatty Hodges was by every reckoning and general acclaim the worst man on the South Downs. There was no telling what kind of mischief he had got Reggie up to.

Noakes and Woollet stared; Reggie stared; they all stared. How could he possibly have known?

"My bees fly everywhere," the old man said. He flexed his neck and rubbed his hands together with a dry rasp. A conjuror with cards, after the ace has been produced. "And they see everyone."

His conclusion, that his bees *told him everything*, he left unspoken. She supposed he feared it would have sounded mad; he was widely held to be quite batty.

"Alas, before you could steal the beloved pet and sole friend of a lonely refugee orphan, you were beaten to the punch by Mr. Shane, the lodger. But as he was about to make off with the bird, Shane was attacked and killed. Now we arrive at the place, or I should say at one place, where the police and I differ. For clearly we also differ as to the advisability of beating the Crown's prisoners, in particular those who have not yet been convicted."

Oh, she thought, what a fine old man this is! Over his bearing, his speech, the tweed suit and tatterdemalion Inverness there hung, like the odor of Turkish shag, all the vanished vigor and rectitude of the Empire.

"Now, sir—" Noakes put in, reproachful; or was it Woollet?

"The police, I say," the old man said, innocent and serene, "seem fairly certain that it was you who surprised Mr. Shane as he was carrying Bruno off, and murdered him. Whereas I believe that it was another, a man—"

The old man's avid gaze now found its way to Reggie's black brogues, bright with the shine she had given them that morning, when the day had promised nothing out of the ordinary.

"—with feet a good deal smaller than your own."

Reggie's face slipped—that disappointed face, smooth as a kneecap. Motionless except where it twisted up at one eyebrow and down at one corner of the mouth. Now, for an instant, it fell away, and he grinned, like a boy. He pulled his great big feet from under the table and stuck them straight out in front of him, marveling as if for the first time at their appalling size.

"That's what I've been telling these two!" he cried. "Yes, all right, another day and I'd have had that bird sold and Fatty paid, and off my back. But the idea wasn't original with me. It's Parkins you should have in here. It was in his wallet that I found Black's card."

"Parkins?" the old man looked to the policemen, who shrugged, and then at her.

"My oldest lodger," she said. "Two years last March." She had never quite trusted Mr. Simon Parkins, she realized, though to all appearances there was nothing in the least exceptionable or shady about him. He rose at the same late hour each morning, went off to study his rolls or rubbings or whatever it was he pored over in the library at Gabriel Park until long past nightfall, and then returned to his room, his lamp, and his supper, warmed over, under a dish.

"Are you in the habit of studyin' the contents of Mr. Parkins's wallet, then, Reg?" said Noakes or Woollett, affably though with a hint of trying too hard, as though he felt the chance to fix Reggie with a murder charge slipping away and hoped to fix him with something else before it was too late.

The old man's head turned toward the policemen with an audible snap.

"I beg you gentlemen also to consider that my days are numbered," he said. "Pray don't ask superfluous questions. Does Parkins take an interest in the bird?"

The question was directed at her.

"Everyone took an interest in Bruno," she said, wondering why she referred to the parrot in the past tense. "Everyone except poor Mr. Shane. Isn't that strange?"

"Parkins takes an interest, all right," Reggie said. The sullenness to which he had at first treated the old man was all gone. "He was always jotting things in his little notebook. Every time the bird started in on those damned numbers."

For the first time since their arrival at the police station, the old man looked truly interested in what was happening. He rose to his feet with none of the moaning and muttering that had attended this action hitherto.

"The numbers!" He laid his hands together palm to palm, arrested between prayer and applause. "Yes! I like that! The bird was wont to repeat numbers."

"All bloody day long."

"Endless series of them," she said, failing even to notice the expletive, though it made one of the policemen wince. She realized now that she had indeed many times seen Parkins pull out a small paper notebook and copy down the numeric arias that emerged from the uncanny clockwork snapping of Bruno's black bill. "One to nine, over and over again, in no particular order."

"And all in *German*," Reggie said.

"And our Mr. Parkins. He is presently employed in what line of work? A commercial traveler, like Richard Shane?"

"He is an architectural historian," she said, noticing that neither Noakes nor Woollett was bothering to write *anything* down. To look at them, those sweating hulks in their blue woolen coats, they might not even have been listening, let alone thinking. Perhaps they felt it was too hot to think. She felt sorry for that intense little inspector from London, Bellows. No wonder he had sent for the old man's help. "He is preparing a monograph on our church."

"And yet he's never there," Reggie said. "Least of all on Sunday."

The detective looked at her for confirmation of this.

"He is presently making a survey of some very old village rolls they keep in the library at Gabriel Park," she said. "I'm afraid I don't really understand it. He's trying to make calculations about the height of the tower in the Middle Ages. It's all—he showed me once. It seemed as much math as architecture."

The old man sank slowly back into his chair, but this time with an air of great abstraction. He was no longer looking at her or at Reggie, or, so far as she could see, at anything in the room. His pipe had long since gone out, and working through a series of automatic steps he relit it, without appearing to notice that he did so. The four human beings sharing the room with him stood or sat, waiting with a remarkable unanimity for him to come to some conclusion. After a full minute of furious smoking, he said, "Parkins," clearly and distinctly, and then he gave a little mumbled speech whose words she couldn't catch. He appeared, she would have said, to be delivering a lecture to himself. Once more he made it up onto his feet, and then headed toward the door of the waiting room, without a backward glance. It was as if he had forgotten them entirely.

"What about me?" Reggie said. "Tell them to let me out, you silly old geezer!"

"Reggie!" She was horrified. Thus far he had said nothing that even remotely resembled an expression of regret over what had happened to Mr. Shane. He had confessed without a jot of shame his plan to steal Bruno from an orphaned little refugee Jew, and to going through the contents of Mr. Parkins's wallet. And now here he was, being rude to the only really worthwhile ally he had ever possessed, apart from her. "For heaven's sake. If you can't see the mess you've got yourself into this time . . ."

The old man turned back from the door, wearing an annoyed little smile.

"Your mother is right," he said. "At this point there is very little evidence to exonerate you, and a good deal of circumstantial evidence that might seem to implicate you. These gentlemen"—he nodded toward Noakes and Woollett—"would be in dereliction of duty if they were to free you. You *appear,* in short, to be quite guilty of murdering Mr. Shane."

Then he pulled on his hunting cap and, with a last nod in her direction, went out.

6

The old man had visited Gabriel Park once before; sometime in the late nineties, that would have been. Then as now it was a question of murder, and there had also been an animal concerned, then—a Siamese cat, painstakingly trained to administer a rare Malay poison with a brush of its whisker against the lips.

The great old house's fortunes appeared in the intervening years to have declined. Before the last war a fire had destroyed the north wing, with its turreted observatory from whose slitted eyelid the Baroness di Sforza—that grand and hideous woman—had leapt to her death, with her precious Siam Queen clutched yowling to her breast. Here and there one still saw blackened timbers jutting from the tall grass like a row of snuffed wicks. The main hall, with all the surrounding pasturelands, had been taken over just before the present war by something called the National Research Dairy; its small, admirably healthy herd of Galloways was the subject of immense skepticism and amusement in the neighborhood.

Forty years ago, the old man recalled, it had needed a regiment of servants to tend the place. Now there was no one to clip the ivy or repaint the window frames, or to replace the lost tiles of the roof, which five years of occupation by the Research Dairy had transformed from a stately defile of chimneys to an upset knitting-basket of aerials and wires. The dairy researchers themselves were seldom seen in town, but it had been observed that a number of them appeared to speak with the accents of far-off Central European lands where, perhaps, the fact that Galloways were beef cattle unsuited to the production of milk was not appreciated. The south wing, severed from the hall by the ostensible milk needs of the nation, languished. One or two of the surviving Curlewes haunted its upper storey. And in its grand old library—the very room in which the old man had, by means of a cleverly placed tin of sardines, unmasked the larcenous feline—Mr. Parkins, and a dozen or so other historians too old or unfit for war, pored over the estate's world-renowned and unparalleled store of tax rolls, account books, and judicial records, kept by the Curlewe family during the seven centuries they had ruled over this part of Sussex.

"I'm sorry, sir," said the young soldier who sat behind a small metal desk in a small metal building at the end of the drive that led up to the house. It was a building of recent and cheap manufacture. One could hardly fail to notice that the soldier wore a Webley in a holster. "But you can't come in without the proper credentials."

The grandson of Sandy Bellows, that dour and tireless exposer of charlatans, displayed his identification card.

"I'm investigating a murder," he said, sounding less sure of himself than either his ancestor or the old man would have liked.

"I heard all about it," said the soldier. He looked, for a moment, truly pained by the thought of Shane's death, long enough for it to strike the old man as curious. Then his face resumed its placid smirk. "But a police badge ain't credentials enough, I'm afraid. National security."

"National—this is a *dairy,* is it not?" the old man cried.

"Milk and milk production are essential to the British war effort," the soldier said brightly.

The old man turned to Sandy Bellows's grandson and saw to his annoyance that the young man seemed to accept this egregious lie. The inspector took a calling card from his wallet and jotted a few words on the reverse.

"Might I ask you to carry this message to Mr. Parkins?" the inspector said. "Or arrange for that to be done?"

The soldier read the message on the back of the card, and considered it for a moment. Then he reached for a black handset and spoke into it softly.

"What did you write?" the old man asked.

The young inspector raised an eyebrow, and it was as if the face of Sandy Bellows were looking out at him across the decades, irritated and amused.

"Can't you guess?" he said.

"Don't be impertinent." And then, out of the side of his mouth, "You wrote, *Richard Shane is dead.*"

I am very much aggrieved to hear that," Francis Parkins declared. They sat in a large room at the back of the south wing, just below the library itself. At one time it had been the servants' dining room; the old man, seeking the poisoner, had conducted interviews with the household staff at this very table. Now the room was being used as a kind of canteen. Tumbled cities of tea tins. Biscuit wrappers. A gas ring for the kettle, and an acrid smell of scorched coffee. The ashtrays had not been emptied. "He was a fine fellow."

"Undoubtedly," the old man said. "He was also a parrot thief."

This Parkins was a long, lean man, dressed like a don in a good tweed suit ill-treated. His head looked too large for his neck, his Adam's apple for his throat, and his hands for his frail white wrists. They were clever hands, supple and expressive. He wore little steel-rimmed spectacles and the lenses caught the light in a way that made it difficult to read his eyes. He gave every appearance of being a cool and settled fellow. There was nothing to be learned from the way Parkins reacted to news of the parrot's disappearance, unless it was something in his reply itself.

"Where is Bruno now?" he said.

He lit a cigarette and tossed the match onto the pile of fag ends in the nearest ashtray. Keeping his face with its illegible eyes on the inspector, he paid not the slightest attention to his companion, a squat, sunburned man who introduced himself, without explanation for his presence at the interview, as Mr. Sackett, managing director of the Research Dairy. Aside from giving his name and title Sackett said nothing. But he lit his cigarette like a soldier, hastily, and listened with an air of one accustomed to seeking flaws in strategies. It was doubtful, thought the old man, he had ever been near an actual cow.

"We had some hope that you might be able to tell us that," the old man said.

"I? You suspect me?"

"Not at all," the inspector said earnestly. "Not for a moment."

"No more," the old man said, "than we believe you to be conducting elaborate mathematical surveys of the height of the church tower in the fourteenth century."

Ah. That one found a chink. The light died in the lenses of his spectacles. Parkins glanced at Mr. Sackett, whose meaty face in its absolute expressionlessness was as eloquent as a fist.

"Gentlemen," Parkins said after a moment. "Inspector. I assure you that I had nothing to do with the death of Mr. Shane, nor with the disappearance of that admirable bird. I have either been in my bed or in the library here for the past two days, though I can offer no proof of that statement, I'm afraid. I can, however, prove to you that my researches are genuine. Let me just run back and fetch my notebook, and I'll show you—"

"What is the current height of the church tower?" the old man said.

"One hundred and thirty-two feet, six inches," said Parkins at once. He smiled. Mr. Sackett tapped the ash from his cigarette.

"And in 1312?"

"I should say seventeen feet shorter, though that remains to be proven."

"A difficult question to settle?"

"Frightfully," Parkins said.

"And doubtless an important one."

"Only to Dryasdusts like me, I'm afraid."

"Bruno, I gather, has provided you with some key insights."

"I don't understand."

"The numbers," Inspector Bellows said. "You keep track of them. Write them down."

The hesitation was brief, but the old man had been lied to by some of the greatest liars of his generation, among whom modesty did not prevent him from including himself. His nearly thirty years spent almost solely in the company of creatures whose honesty could not be impeached seemed to have had no ill effects on the sensitivity of his instrument. Parkins was lying his head off.

"Merely for my own amusement," Parkins said. "There's nothing in them. Just a lot of nonsense."

A delicate, inexorable lattice of inferences began to assemble themselves, like a crystal, in the old man's mind, shivering, catching the light in glints and surmises. It was the deepest pleasure life could afford, this deductive crystallization, this paroxysm of guesswork, and one that he had lived without for a terribly long time.

"What does Bruno know?" he said. "Whose numbers was he taught to repeat?"

"I'm afraid we don't concern ourselves with such questions here," Mr. Sackett said quietly.

"Am I to understand," the old man said, "that Mr. Parkins is an employee, or as it were a fellow, of your facility, Mr. Sackett? Is there some vital connection between Norman church architecture and the milking of beef cattle of which I am unaware?"

The inspector sought valiantly to cover his laughter with a cough. Mr. Sackett frowned.

"Detective Inspector Bellows," Sackett said, his voice softer than ever. "I wonder if I might have a word with you."

Bellows nodded and they stood up and went out into the

hall. Just before he left the room, Mr. Sackett turned and aimed a warning look at Mr. Parkins, whose cheeks colored.

"I take it I am about to be warned off," the old man said.

But the rime of light had returned to the lenses of Mr. Parkins's spectacles. He smiled thinly. The tap dripped into the basin; a cigarette in one of the choked ashtrays burned to the filter and filled the room with an acrid smell of hair. A moment later the inspector came back into the room, alone.

"Thank you, Mr. Parkins. You may go," he said, then turned to the old man, an apology in his expression, his voice imprinted, as it were, with an echo of Mr. Sackett's hard-edged whisper of command. "We're all finished here."

An hour later, Reggie Panicker was released, with all charges against him dropped, and the next day, at the inquest, the death of Richard Woolsey Shane was officially ruled to have been the result of an accident whose nature was not then or afterward specified.

7

The bees did speak to him, after a fashion. The featureless drone, the sonic blank that others heard was to him a shifting narrative, rich, inflected, variable, and distinct as the separate stones of a featureless gray shingle, and he moved along the sound, tending to his hives like a beachcomber, stooped and marveling. It meant nothing, of course—he wasn't as batty as all that—but this did not imply, not at all, that the song had no meaning. It was the song of a city, a city as far from London as London was from heaven or Rangoon, a city in which all did precisely what they were supposed to do, in the way that had been prescribed by their most remote and venerable ancestors. A city in which gems, gold ingots, letters of credit, or secret naval plans were never stolen, in which long-lost second sons and ne'er-do-well first husbands did not turn up from the Wawoora Valley or the Rand with some clever backwoods trick for scaring an old moneybags out of his wits. No stabbings, garrotings, beatings, shootings; almost no violence at all, apart from the occasional regicide. All of the death in the city of the bees had been scheduled, provided for, tens of millions of years ago; each death as it occurred was translated, efficiently and immediately, into more life for the hive.

It was the sort of city in which a man who had earned his keep among murderers and ruffians might choose to pass the remainder of his days, listening to its song, as a young man fresh to Paris or New York or Rome (or even, as he still dimly recalled, London) stood on a balcony, at the window of a bedsit, on the roof of a tenement house, listening to the rumble of traffic and the fanfare of horns, and feeling that he was hearing the music of his own mysterious destiny.

Between the epic of the bees and the rasp of his own respiration within the tent of his protective netting, he failed to hear, as he had failed to anticipate, the long black saloon car that turned up the day after his interview with Parkins. It was not until the man from London was ten feet behind him that the old man turned. Easy prey, he thought, disgusted with himself. Fortunate, really, that all one's enemies are dead.

The man from London was dressed like a cabinet minister but he moved like a cashiered soldier. Broad-chested, fair-haired, squinting as against a hostile sun, a curious shuffling motion in his left foot, in its good Cleverley

brogue, as he came toward the hives. Old enough to have ac-
cumulated a score of enemies, certainly, but not yet old
enough to have outlived them all. His driver waited by the
car with its London plates and its slitted blackout headlights
that echoed the sun-blasted squint of its passenger.

"Do they ever sting you?" the man from London said.

"Constantly."

"Does it hurt?"

The old man raised the netting, so that he would not
have to waste a perfectly good yes on such a fatuous question. The man from London concealed the traces of a smile
in his graying blond mustache.

"Suppose it would," he said. "Like honey, do you?"

"Not particularly, no," said the old man.

The man from London appeared to be a little surprised
by this reply, then nodded and confessed that he was not terribly fond of honey himself.

"Know who I am?" he said, after a moment.

"Genus and species," the old man said. He lifted a hand
to the veil of net as if to lower it again. Then he pulled off
the hat entirely, and tucked it under his arm. "You'd better
come inside."

The man from London took the chair by the window,
and made a discreet attempt to crank an inch or two of fresh
air into the room. It was the least comfortable chair in the
cottage, combining all the worst qualities of a sawhorse and
a church pew, but the old man was under no illusion about

the odor in the room. Not that he could smell it himself, any more than a bear, or for that matter an ogre, noticed or minded the stench of his own dark den.

"I can offer you a cup of tea," he said, though in fact he was not entirely certain that he could. "I believe my supply dates from the early nineteen thirties. I don't know, Colonel, whether tea leaves turn bitter with time or lose their flavor entirely but I feel reasonably certain that mine have met their fate. Am I right? It is Colonel?"

"Threadneedle."

"Colonel Threadneedle. Cavalryman?"

"Mounted infantry. Lennox Highlanders."

"Ah. Whisky, then."

The proposal was offered and accepted in the spirit of hostile good humor that had so far characterized his dealings with the intelligence officer, but at once he was racked with anxiety as to whether the whisky he had suggested in such a cavalier fashion had been drunk years before, in other lodgings, had perhaps evaporated or turned to a tarry paste, was not whisky to begin with, had ever existed at all. Five minutes' speleology in the nether regions of the corner cabinet produced a bottle of Glenmorangie, buried in a layer of dust that might have repelled a Schliemann. He stood, trembling with relief, and brushed the sweat from his brow with the back of a cardiganned arm. As a young man, to be warned off from pursuing an investigation had been a positive development, a landmark on the road to solution, and more than this, a thrill.

"Found it!" he cried.

He spilled a generous amount into a reasonably clean glass and handed it to the man from London, then lowered himself into his armchair. The memory of the taste of scotch was in his mouth like the smell of burning leaves lingering on a woolen scarf. But the cords that held him together were so few and threadbare that he feared to loosen them.

"This country," the colonel began. "Too quick to forgive its enemies and too hasty to forget its old friends." He took a deep whiff of the two inches of scotch in his glass, as if to scour his nostrils, then drained half. He grunted, in a way that was perhaps involuntary, and gave a wistful sigh of contentment: the passing years were, in every other respect, so cruel. "That at least is my view."

"I hope that I was of some little service, here and there, over the years."

"It was felt," the colonel began, "that you were entitled to an explanation."

"That's very kind."

"The boy is the son of a Dr. Julius Steinman, Berlin physician. Name means nothing to me, but in psychiatric circles . . ." He made a face to indicate his judgment of psychiatrists and their opinions. The old man appreciated but did not share the prejudice; as doctors, no doubt, psychiatrists left something to be desired, but they often made fine detectives. "Apparently the man had some success treating certain forms of sleep disorders. God knows how. Drugs, I'd wager. At any rate, the boy and his parents were spared deportation in 1938. Taken off the train at the last moment, I gather."

"Someone having nightmares," the old man said.

"Shouldn't wonder."

"Someone involved with codes and ciphers."

" 'Involved' with something very secret, at any rate." He gazed fondly at the last inch of whisky in his glass, then bade it farewell. "Held on to his personal Jew doctor for as long as he could. Keeping the bad dreams at bay. Quartered with him in some kind of secret facility or camp. The whole family. Wife, boy, parrot."

"Where the parrot, with all the stealth and craft his breed is known for, proceeded to commit to memory the cipher keys for the Kriegsmarine."

The man from London appreciated the sarcasm slightly less, perhaps, than he had the scotch.

"They were taught to him, naturally," he said. "That's the theory, at any rate. This Parkins fellow has been sitting on it for months, apparently. As soon as we learned of it—"

"You tried to get Reggie Panicker to steal it for you, and sell it to this Mr. Black, who, I suppose, is in your employ."

"Not to my knowledge," the man from London said, and in his tone was the polite suggestion that the ambit of this knowledge well sufficed any purpose of the old man's. "And you're wrong about the Panicker lad. We had nothing to do with that."

"And you don't care who killed your Mr. Shane."

"Oh, we care. Yes, indeed. Shane was a fine man. A skilled operative. His death is most disturbing, not least for its clear implication that someone was sent to retrieve this bird." He did not seem to feel it necessary to suggest who this someone might have been sent by. "He may be lying low in the surrounding countryside. He may be a sleeper, someone who's been here living and working in the village since long before the war began. Or he may be halfway across the North Sea at this moment, on his way home."

"Or he may be in his study in the vicarage, hard at work on a sermon for this Sunday. A sermon whose text is taken from the second chapter of Hosea, verses one through three."

"Perhaps," the man from London said with a dry cough that he seemed to intend to serve as proxy for an actual laugh. "Your young friend the inspector is onto the father now."

"Yes, he would be."

"But that seems unlikely. Chap grows roses, doesn't he?"

"A bitter, disappointed, and jealous man kills the man he believes to be his wife's lover, this you consider to be un-likely. A murderous Nazi spy with orders to abduct a parrot, on the other hand—"

"Yes, well." The colonel peered into the empty glass of whisky, cheeks coloring as if with chagrin. "It's just that, given the opportunity, we would do the same thing, wouldn't we?" Some inward slackening of the cords seemed to have taken place in the colonel, but the old man doubted that the fault lay in a dusty glass of scotch. He had known the flower of British intelligence, from the days of the Great Game through the first echoes of the guns of Mons. In the end their trade boiled down to purest mirror work: inversions and reflections, echoes. And there was always something dispiriting about the things one saw in a looking glass. "If *they* had a parrot stuffed to the wingtips with *our* naval cipher, we would certainly make every effort to get it back." The colonel looked up at the old man with a smile that mocked himself and the ministry that employed him. "Or see it roasted on a spit."

He rose from the very hard chair with a cracking of the timbers of his soldierly frame. Then with a last longing look at the bottle of scotch, he went to the door.

"This is a war we are trying extremely hard not to lose," he said. "A learned parrot would be far from the most preposterous thing for it to hinge upon."

"I have promised to find Bruno," the old man said. "And so I shall."

"Should you manage the trick," the colonel said. A long shaft of the summer afternoon reached into the house as he opened the door. The old man could hear the chant of the bees in their cities. The light itself was the color of honey. In the dooryard the driver awoke from his drowse, and the engine of the saloon car rumbled to life. "Thanks of a grateful nation and so forth."

"I shall return him to the *boy*."

This came out more petulant than the old man would have liked, reedy and cracked, and he regretted having said it. It could not be regarded by his visitor even as the hollow bravado of an old codger.

The man from London frowned, and let out a sigh that might have been embittered or admiring. Then the colonel shook his head once, firmly, in a way that was ordinarily, the old man imagined, sufficient to any nullifying purpose that might arise in the course of a day's work. The colonel took out a scrap of paper and the chewed blue stub of a pencil. He scrawled a number on the back of the scrap and then neatly poked it into a crack in the warped wooden frame of the door. Just before he went out, he turned back and looked at the old man, wearing an oddly dreamy expression.

"What's the taste of parrot meat, I wonder?" he said.

8

The hives were a row of gabled boxes on the south side of the cottage, miniature pagodas, white and stepped as wedding cakes. One of the colonies dated from 1926; in his thoughts it was always the "Old Hive." The "Old Hive" had been mothered and ruled by generations of strong, prolific queens. It was as ancient to the old man as Britain itself, as the chalk bones of the South Downs. And now, as in each of the seventeen preceding summers, the time had come to ravish it of its honey.

On the morning proposed for the extraction, he read J.G. Digges until four, then slept fitfully for an hour until he knew that it was time to get up. He had never relied on alarm clocks. He was a lifelong light sleeper, and in his dotage an outright insomniac. When he did sleep, his dreams were puzzles and algebra problems, troubling his rest. He preferred on the whole to be awake.

Everything took longer than it ought to have taken—ablutions, coffee, priming the first pipe of the day. He had never really learned to cook, and the latest Satterlee girl who looked after him would not be in until seven. By then he would be deeply at work on the hives. So he ate nothing. Even without bothering about breakfast, however, he was annoyed to find that by the time he had fought the daily battle in the lavatory, washed his lean old limbs, fastened all the zips of his bee suit, pulled on his rubber-soled boots, and donned his bee hat, the sun was already well up and blazing in the sky. It was going to be a hot day, and hot bees were discontented bees. For now at least there was still a nocturnal chill in the air, fog on the high ground, a heavy taste of the sea. So he wasted another five minutes enjoying his pipe. The morning cool, the burning shag, the drowse of the late summer, honey-sated bees: until this recent adventure of the learned parrot these were the pleasures of his life. They were animal pleasures, as he recognized.

Such things had once meant very little to him.

The soles of his boots squeaked in the grass as he went to the shed to fetch his housebreaking tools, and they squeaked as he limped across to the hives. He could smell the ointment tang of heather honey from halfway across the hiveyard. A good summer for heather this year. The Satterlees would be pleased; by ancient arrangement the family sold the yield of his hives, and kept the profits, and heather honey fetched four or five times the price of a common blend.

At last he stood before the "Old Hive," holding his fuming board and the stoppered bottle of benzaldehyde. The hive gave off an air of doomed contentment, like a city sleeping it off on the day after carnival, contemplated from a hilltop by an army of Huns. The old man drew a deep chestful of smoke and then lowered himself to the ground, leaning on the fuming board for balance. A couple of workers loitered outside the round portal of the city.

"Morning, ladies," he said; or perhaps he merely thought it.

He put his lips to the entrance hole and blew in a rank rich exhalation of mundungus. He had bred a commendable docility into his stock but when you came to steal their honey it was best not to take any chances. The shag he favored possessed remarkable powers of tranquilization; *The British Bee Journal* had published his notes on the subject.

He ratcheted himself to his feet and prepared to remove the super, with its fat, waxy combs. This was not a task he relished; the supers got heavier every year. It took no effort to imagine losing his footing on the way to the covered porch around the back of the cottage where he ran the extractor: the snap of a critical bone, the splintered frames of honey spilt on the ground. He did not fear death exactly, but he had evaded it for so many years that it had come to seem

The hive gave off air of doomed contentment

formidable simply by virtue of that long act of evasion. In particular he feared dying in some undignified way, on the jakes or with his face in the porridge.

Carefully he let his pipe go out and then tucked it into the wide pocket of his bee suit alongside his matches and pouch of tobacco. Benzoic aldehyde was only moderately flammable, but the prospect of setting himself on fire with his own pipe conformed to his worst ideas of the indignity that death would one day visit upon him. With the pipe out of the way, he unstoppered the brown glass bottle, and his organ of smell was overwhelmed, all but undone, by a strident blast of marzipan. He sprinkled the stuff liberally on the felt batting of the fuming board. Then he reached for the peaked roof of the hive and lifted it off. Quickly, nearly dropping it, he laid it on the ground and turned back to the comb, the beautiful comb, each cell of it sealed with a wax cap of sturdy bee manufacture. It had the strange pallor of heather honeycomb, an intense whiteness, white as death or a gardenia. He admired it. Here and there a bee surprised at its business contemplated the meaning of the disturbance, the sudden burst of daylight. One, a heroine of her people, rose at once into the air to attack him. If she stung him, he didn't remark it; he had long since grown habituated to the stings. He settled the fuming board down over the pale expanse of comb and hoisted the roof back into place over it. In a few minutes the hated stench of the aldehyde would have driven any bees still hanging about the comb down to the next level in the hive.

When the veil of his bee hat was lowered he generally could hear nothing apart from the breathing and the mumble of bees. But he had not troubled with the veil, with the bees so slow and fat, and so he chanced to hear the stifled cry behind him. It was more of a gasp than a cry, really, brief and disappointed. At first he thought it must be the Satterlee girl but when he turned he saw the boy standing by the garden shed, sucking on the back of his hand. He was wearing the same short pants and clean, pressed shirt as on the day of their first encounter, but standing there without the parrot he struck the old man as looking glaringly bereft.

The old man grinned. "Hurts, don't it?"

The boy nodded slowly, too surprised or in too much pain to feign lack of understanding. The old man ambled over to him, shaking his head.

"What a singularly *unlucky* boy you are," he said. "Let's have a look."

He took hold of the boy's hand. On the back, just below the wrist, a puffy nipple of flesh, tipped with the black filament of the barb. The old man took a matchbox from the zip pocket of his bee suit, poked out the tray of matches. Cupping the tray in his left hand, with his right he flattened the outer sleeve of the matchbox. Then, using an edge of the flattened bit of cardboard, he scraped the sting out of the boy's hand. The boy wept freely during this procedure.

"Mustn't yank them out," he told the boy with a sharpness he did not entirely intend. He was aware of the existence of a vocabulary for the consolation of sorrowing children, but it was one he had never troubled to learn. Boys had served him well over the years—but that was in another century!—extending the reach of his eyes and ears, passing invisibly into dark lanes and courtyards where his own presence would have drawn undue attention, slipping over transoms, through the back doors of hostile alehouses, in and out of the stable yards of crooked horse trainers. And in his own lofty jocular way he had spoken to and even, carelessly, cared for those boys. But they were a different species of boy entirely, ragged, rude, pinched and avid, holes in their shoes, holes for eyes, boys disciplined by hunger and poverty to display the narrowest possible spectrum of human emotion. They would have sooner drunk lye than allowed themselves to be seen to shed a tear. "Only spreads the venom."

The barb tumbled free; the boy took back his hand and studied the pink histamine swell. Then he returned his hand to the solace of his mouth. There was something about the sight of the mute boy sucking on the back of his hand that enraged the old man. He allowed a desire to slap the boy's cheek thrill him for a moment.

"Wait a moment," he said. "Not like that."

Fumbling, rage and arthritis crippling his fingers, he tried to reassemble the components of the matchbox. The little drawer tipped and scattered matches on the ground. The old man swore. Then, at once with deliberateness and out of some wild impulse he swore a second time, vilely, in

German. The agreeably rancid syllables escaped his lips with an audible smack of pleasure.

The boy unkissed the fiery back of his hand. A wicked look animated the wide somber gaze, a parrot gleam of hard amusement that had from time to time, in that vanished nineteenth century, flared in the hard hollow eyes of those ragged urchin irregulars. The boy unburdened the old man of the sundered halves of matchbox, knelt down, quickly gathered up the strewn matchsticks, and tucked them neatly into their berth. He passed the box back to the old man, who restored it to the zip pocket of his bee suit and took out the pouch of shag. He removed a pinch, showering rank confetti on the ground. Out came his ogre tongue, pointed and fissured. A dab of his dragon saliva. Then he held out his hand to the boy.

"Here," the old man said as gently as he could manage. He had a feeling that it was none too gently. The boy understood. He passed his wounded hand to the old man, his face at once grave and expectant, as if they were about to seal some boyish pact in pinpricks of blood or palms anointed with sacrosanct saliva. The old man laid the moist gob of tobacco against the welt. He took the boy's other hand and pressed the palm against the bee sting and the knot of tobacco. "Like this. Hold it there."

The boy obeyed while the old man labored to remove the fuming board from the uppermost super. He hoped he had not left it to sit too long; prolonged exposure to the fumes could queer the flavor of the honey. Setting the board to one side he grasped the ends of the honey-laden super and staggered a few steps toward the extracting porch, working feverishly, and with a desperation that saddened him, not to appear to be staggering. His effort failed to fool the boy. There was a squeak of rubber soles in the grass and then the boy was there, beside him, taking hold of one end of the rectangular frame of the super with the injured hand—the welt appeared already to have begun to subside.

Together they made their way to the porch. The boy's eyes were not on the old man but on the air around him, darting, wary, fearing a further attack. As the old man struggled to get the screened door open the weight of the frame shifted inexorably onto the boy. He bore it. They lumbered into the porch, where the centrifuge, with its great, toothed hand crank, waited, bearing the patient reproachful air of all idle farm machinery. Even open as it was, a deep, vinegar gloom hung about the porch from bygone years of harvest. They laid the tray with its weirdly radiant cargo of wax on a clean bedsheet and started back toward the hives.

Laboring alone—his way, preferred and inevitable, for the past thirty years it might have taken him until well past dark to finish the job of removing the supers one by one from the six hives, two supers per hive; cutting out the frames of comb; slicing off the wax caps with the heated blade of a bread knife; loading dripping sections of cut comb into the extractor and working the crank until all the honey that could be persuaded to abandon the combs had been drained off, by various operations of centrifugal force and gravity, into the settling jars; ensuring that the porch was screened and sealed against counterraids; and returning the ravaged supers to the hives. With the help of Linus Steinman, increasingly competent as the day wore on, intelligent and handy and blessedly, staunchly, wonderfully free of conversation, he completed the work just after four in the afternoon. They stood together in the screened porch, in the dense, foul reek—like the atmosphere of a planet of fermentation and decay, like the planet Venus in all its purported rank inhospitable riot—of honey. At the stilling of the centrifuge the porch, the farmstead, this vale in the lee of a hillside, the immense bowl of tedious green country around them seemed to fill with a thick and gummy mass of silence.

All at once the comfort of their mutual labor abandoned them. They regarded each other.

The boy had something he wanted to say. He felt his pockets, fingers sticking with a whispery rasp to the fabric of short trousers, and shirt. His bit of pencil turned up in the seat pocket of his short trousers, but as the search for the pad continued without issue a crease appeared in the boy's domed brow. He patted himself up and down until filaments of honey floss formed between his fingertips and pockets, coating him in a gossamer down. The old man watched helpless as the boy, with mounting agitation, spun threads of loss from his palms and fingertips. Doubtless the pad, in the continued absence of Bruno, was all that remained to him in the way of a companion to his thoughts.

"Perhaps you dropped it by the hives," the old man suggested, and as he said the words he heard both the note of genuine comfort that he had, at last, managed to work into them; and the utter adult hollowness of the hope that they extended.

Duly they tramped out across the hiveyard where the old man, his joints ablaze, his muscles quivering, managed to get his clattering remains down onto the ground. With his accustomed canine aplomb he combed the yard for the cheap pasteboard-and-pulp remnant of the lost boy's voice. From the low angle of his search the six hives loomed white and solemn in the late sunlight as a street of temples in Lucknow or Hong Kong. While he crawled on hands and knees the possibility of his dying thus recurred to him, and he found to his pleasure that no shadow of indignity darkened the prospect. Long life wore away everything that was not essential. Some old men finished their lives as little more than the sum total of their memories, others as nothing but a pair of grasping pincers, or a set of bitter axioms proven. It would please him well enough to amount to no more in the end than a single great organ of detection, reaching into blankness for a clue.

At last, however, he was forced to concede that there was nothing to be found. When he rose unsteadily to his feet, the throbbing of his joints was like a universal sentiment of loss, the action on his bones of certain things' implacable resistance, once lost, to ever being found. Heavily, as if fetching it from far across the North Sea, the boy produced a sigh. The old man stood, shrugging. With the consciousness of failure, a gray shadow seemed to steal over his senses as if, steady as a cloud, a great obstructing satellite were scudding across the face of the sun. Meaning drained from the world like light fleeing the operation of an eclipse. The vast body of experience and lore, of corollaries and observed results, of which he felt himself the master, was at a stroke rendered useless. The world around him was a page of alien text. A row of white cubes from which there escaped a mysterious drone of lamentation. A boy in a glowing miasma of threads, his staring face flat and edged with shadow as if cut from paper and pasted against the sky. A breeze drawing rippling portraits of emptiness in the pale green tips of the grass.

The old man brought a fist to his lips and pressed it there, fighting down a hot spike of nausea. His attempt to reassure himself with the dim recollection that such eclipses had happened before was arrested by the counter-recollection that they were coming more frequently now.

Linus Steinman smiled. From some unplumbed pocket or lining the boy had produced a scrap of card. The occluding moon rolled on; the world was dazzled once more with sense and light and the marvelous vanity of meaning. The old man's eyes filmed with shameful tears as, relieved, he watched the boy scribble a brief query on the bit of paper he had found. He came across the grass and, a question in his eyes, handed the old man the torn scrap of ecru laid.

"Leg ov red," the old man read. He felt strongly that he ought to understand this communication but the sense of it lay just beyond his grasp. Perhaps his breaking-down brain had failed, this time, to make a full recovery from its recent lapse. An invocation, perhaps, illiterate and broken, of the pink-tinged talons of the vanished African gray? Or—

The scrap slipped from the old man's fingers and spun fluttering to the ground. The old man stooped, grunting, to retrieve it, and when he picked it up again found on the reverse of the scrap two words and a numeral, written not in the boy's crooked graphite scratch but in the bold hand of an adult, in black ink with a narrow nib. It was the address, in Club Row, of Mr. Jos. Black, Dealer in Rare and Exotic Birds.

"Where did you get this paper?" the old man said.

The boy took back the card and, under the address, scrawled the single word: BLAK.

"He was here? You spoke to him?"

The boy nodded.

"I see," the old man said. "I see that I must go up to London."

9

Mr. Panicker nearly ran him down.

In fine weather, and driven by a man as sober as the tenor of his profession demanded, the Panicker vehicle, small, Belgian, ancient, ill-used by the son of its current owner and retaining few of its original constituent parts, was difficult to govern. Its tiny windscreen and broken left headlamp lent it a squinting, groping aspect, like that of a drowning sinner seeking an allegorical lifeline. Its steering mechanism, as was perhaps fitting, relied to a large degree on the steady application of prayer. Its brakes, though it was blasphemy to say, may have lain beyond the help even of divine intercession. On the whole in its unfitness, shabbiness, and supreme air of steady and irremediable poverty it neatly symbolized, in his own personal view, all that was germane to the life of the man who—far from professionally sober and caught up in a gust of inward turbulence nearly as profound as that which on this cold, wet, blustery, thoroughly English summer morning buffeted the sad tan Imperia from one side to the other of the London road—found himself, his foot pumping madly at the hopeless brake pedal, the single wiper smearing and revising its translucent arc of murk across the windscreen, on the brink of committing vehicular manslaughter.

At first, seeing nothing but a flapping shadow, a tumbling sheet of oilcloth blown from on top of some farmer's woodpile, empty and uninhabited, he prepared to plunge straight through it and trust in the ironic fortune that had ever been his to fathom. Then, just as the furling blanket of his destiny was about to swallow him, the sheet resolved itself into a cloak and claws, a great bat of brown tweed flapping toward him. It was a man, the old man, the mad old beekeeper, lurching into the road with his long pale face, arms awhirl. A huge frantic hawk moth fluttering into his path. Mr. Panicker wrenched the wheel to the left. The open bottle, purloined from his wretched son, that until now had been the sole companion of his turmoil flew from its perch on the seat beside him and smacked against the glove compartment, scattering brandy as it swung through the air like an aspergillum. With a palpable sense of freedom, as if at last it had attained the state to which, throughout its meager career of puttering, shivering, creeping, and stalling, it had

long aspired, the Imperia described a series of broad, balletic loops across the London road, each linked, in a circular pattern, to the last, leaving a child's drawing of a daisy half drawn in streaks on the slick black macadam. It was at this point that Mr. Panicker's relations with his deity once again demonstrated their long-standing sardonic trend. The car abandoned or perhaps lost interest in its escapade and came to a juddering stop some twenty feet farther along the road than it had begun, its bonnet directed faithfully toward London, engine rumbling, lone headlamp peering through the falling rain, as if it had received a scolding for its antics and was now prepared to continue on its humble way. His process of thought, hitherto a chaotic combustion fueled by twin reservoirs of unaccustomed bibulousness and a kind of jolly rage, also appeared to have come juddering to a halt. Where was he going, what was he doing? Had he truly, at long last, escaped? Could one simply roll one's trousers in a grip and walk out?

The passenger door flew open. With a howl of wind and trailing a retinue of raindrops the old man billowed into the car. He pulled the door shut behind him and shook himself in his Inverness like a lean dank dog.

"Thanks," he said curtly. He turned his horrible bright gaze on his rescuer, on the upended bottle of brandy, on the torn seat-leather and exposed wires and peeling dashboard, on the very state, or so it seemed to Mr. Panicker, of his sodden and astonished soul. His long flared nostrils felt out each scattered fleck of brandy in the air. "Good morning to you."

Mr. Panicker understood that he was expected now to engage the forward gear and proceed to London, conveying thither, as if they had prearranged it, his new passenger and his smell of wet wool and tobacco. Yet he could not seem to bring himself to do so. So profound had his unconscious identification with the 1927 Imperia become that he felt now as if this large, damp old man had intruded directly into the glum sanctity of his own rattletrap skull.

The engine as if with a sigh settled into a patient idle. His passenger seemed to interpret Mr. Panicker's immobility and silence as a request for explanation, which, in a manner of speaking, Mr. Panicker supposed, it was.

"Rail service 'interrupted,'" the old man said dryly. "Troop movements, I imagine. Reinforcements to Mortain, no doubt. I gather the fighting there has turned thick. In any case, I have no way to reach London by rail today, and yet I find myself very much obliged to go."

He peered forward, looking into the foot-well between his mud-caked boots, high-lacing, thick-ribbed old ammunition boots of the sort that had marched on Khartoum and Bloemfontein. With a grunt, and a creaking of bones that Mr. Panicker found quite alarming, he reached forward and retrieved the bottle of brandy, and with it the tiny corked stopper that had popped out and rolled from view soon after his departure—clandestine if hardly stealthy—from the vicarage. The old man sniffed at the neck of the bottle, and grimaced, raising an eyebrow. Then, with his facial features settled into an expression so deadpan that it could not fail to register as mocking, he proffered the bottle to Mr. Panicker.

Mr. Panicker shook his head dumbly and engaged the clutch. The old man replaced the stopper on the bottle. And they set off for the city through the rain.

They drove in silence for a long while as Mr. Panicker, finding his tank of rage drained and his drunkenness subsiding, lapsed into a funk of baffled embarrassment at his own recent behavior. He had always been, supremely and if nothing else, a man whose acts and opinions were characterized by rectitude, by that careful absence of surprisingness that he had been taught, years before at the seminary in Kottayam, to prize among the signal virtues of a successful vicar. The silence, the deep elderly sighs and occasional sidewise glances of his unwanted passenger struck him as prelude to an inevitable request for explanation.

"I suppose you're wondering . . . ?" he began, hands gripping the wheel, hunching forward to bring his face nearer the windscreen.

"Yes?"

He decided—the idea appeared full and lustrous in his imagination as if tipped in by an artful hand—to tell the old man that he was on his way to London to attend a synod, entirely fictitious, of the Anglican clergy of southeastern England. This would account for the grip on the rear bench, beside the cans of precious petrol, packed for a journey of some two or three days. Yes, a synod at Church House. He would be staying at the Crampton, with its more than adequate restaurant. There was to be a series of thoughtful discussions, in the morning, of questions of liturgy, followed by lunch, and then in the afternoon a series of more practical seminars devoted to preparing the ministry to enter the postwar period. The Right Reverend Stackhouse-Hall, Archdeacon of Bromley, would address, with his usual learned good humor, the unexpected stresses that would naturally present themselves to families as they welcomed soldier fathers and husbands home. As Mr. Panicker continued to burnish and amplify his excuse, its appeal to him increased, and he found himself strangely cheered by its prospect.

"I perceive that I have intruded on you in a difficult time, Mr. Panicker," the old man said.

With a wistful gesture Mr. Panicker swept the conference hall, hotel, restaurant, a set of matchstick towers, from the tabletop of his fancy. He was a faithless middle-aged minister, drunk and in flight from the ruin of his life.

"Oh, no, I . . ." Mr. Panicker began, but then found that he was unable to continue, his throat constricted and his eyes stung with the imminence of tears. There are times, as he well knew, when merely having our sorrow guessed at could itself be a kind of rude consolation.

"It's really quite remarkable that I should so literally

have crossed your path this morning. For the business that brings me to London is intimately connected with your own household, sir."

So that was it. Though the police had exonerated, or at least called off their investigation of his son in the murder of that chair-straddling traveler in teat-yanking machinery, the shadow of doubt had not been lifted from Mr. Panicker's own consideration of the crime. The possibility of Reggie's guilt was a matter of shame to Mr. Panicker, as was nearly everything that touched in some way or another on his son, but this time his shame was compounded by the intimate knowledge that Richard Shane's brutal murder in the road behind the vicarage had echoed, in outline and particulars, the secret trend of his own darkest imaginings. When the detective inspector, Bellows, had called last week, the implication of the visit, couched though the questions were in terms of utmost circumspection, had been unmistakable. He himself, Kumbhampoika Thomas Panicker, public proponent and living symbol of the gentle but unyielding love of the Lord, stood credibly under suspicion of having killed a man—out of jealousy. And he could not help feeling that his desire to do so—that anger which set his hands trembling whenever a word of Shane's induced the stunning miracle of a smile on his wife's face—had somehow escaped his heart, like a gas, and fatally poisoned his son's, already diseased.

"It was my understanding . . . Reggie . . . the police said . . ."

It struck him now that the old man and he had not "crossed paths" at all. He was still under investigation, and now the police had enlisted this ancient veteran; or perhaps the fantastical coot had put himself, half dementedly, on the case.

"Tell me," the old man said, and the prosecutorial lilt in his voice confirmed all of Mr. Panicker's fears. "Have you remarked, or encountered personally, any strangers around the vicarage of late?"

"Strangers? I don't—"

"This would be a chap from London, likely I should say an older man, perhaps a Jew. Man by the name of Black."

"The dealer in birds," Mr. Panicker said. "They found his card in Reggie's pocket."

"I have reason to believe that he has recently paid a visit to your young lodger, Master Steinman."

"Paid a visit?" The boy of course received no visitors at all, apart from Martin Kalb. "Not so far as I—"

"Clearly, as I have suspected from the beginning, Mr. Black is indeed aware of our Bruno's existence, and of his remarkable abilities. This recent attempt directly to contact Master Steinman suggests that Black had received no communication from any of his alleged agents in this affair, and knew nothing of the bird's disappearance. Perhaps, indeed, it was in despair of ever receiving such a communication that he paid a clandestine visit to the boy, seeking to arrange for its sale, or perhaps to steal it himself. In any event, I intend to put some rather direct questions to Mr. Joseph Black of Club Row. Otherwise I shall never arrive at a final disposition of the bird's whereabouts."

"The bird," Mr. Panicker repeated, slowing the car. They were approaching East Grinstead, where the police had set up a checkpoint, and the traffic had already begun to back up. The old man had been correct then, in his surmise about increased military activity; security had been tightened. "You are looking for the *bird*."

The old man turned to him, an eyebrow raised, as if something about Mr. Panicker struck him as unfortunate or reproachable.

"Aren't *you*?" he said. "It seems to me that anyone charged with acting in loco parentis would view the disappearance of such a beloved and remarkable animal . . ."

"Yes, yes of course," Mr. Panicker said. "We are all very . . . the boy has been . . . inconsolable."

In fact the bird had entered Mr. Panicker's thoughts in the two weeks since its disappearance only as a kind of grim mental aftereffect of the scenes of violence and bloodshed, of cuckoldry revenged and indignity repaid, that had characterized his imaginings during the brief tenancy at the vicarage of the damned Mr. Shane. For Mr. Panicker was certain that Bruno the parrot was dead, and dead furthermore in some particularly gruesome or violent manner. Despite its wild origin in, as his consultation of the "P" volume of the *Encyclopedia Britannica* had informed him, the tropical regions of Africa, Bruno was a house bird, cultivated and tamed. In the open country, in the hands of ruffians, surely it would come to grief. He envisioned the bird's staring ink-pool eye as its neck was wrung; saw its body tossed, broken, trailing feathers and fluff, into a dustbin or gutter; saw it torn apart by stoats; tangled in telegraph wires. The horror of these visions came somewhat as a surprise to Mr. Panicker, given that—as was not the case with the late Dick Shane, whom his imagination had consigned to similar fates—he had always esteemed the bird very highly. In all the turmoil of the murder investigation, the foul tide of neighborhood gossip, and the drawing, at long last, of the final synthesis in the lifelong syllogism of disappointment that was his marriage to Ginny Stallard, these irruptions of blood-bright avian mayhem were the sole intrusions of the matter of the missing bird into his consciousness. Now for the first time (and here the sense of shame he felt was deeper and more searing than anything his marriage, his career, or the misbehavior of his unfortunate son had ever or could ever have inspired in him) he spared a thought—a small, frail, sober-eyed, wordless, Linus Steinman–sized thought—for the boy who had lost his only friend.

"In all the recent confusion . . ." the old man offered helpfully. And then, "No doubt your pastoral duties and obligations . . ."

"No," Mr. Panicker said. All at once he felt himself sober and calm, and, at the same time a spasm of absurd gratitude seized him. "Of course not."

They had reached the checkpoint. A pair of uniformed policemen approached the Imperia, one on either side. Mr. Panicker rolled down his window, assisting the process as was necessary with a series of sharp tugs on the upper edge of the glass.

"Good morning, sir. May I ask your reason for traveling to London?"

"Reason?"

Mr. Panicker looked at the old man, who looked back at him with a steady humorous unconcern.

"Yes," Mr. Panicker said. "Oh. Yes. Well, we've, er, come to look for a parrot, haven't we?"

M r. Panicker's wife, ruefully true to her married name, suffered from gephyrophobia, the morbid fear of crossing bridges. When a car, bus, or train in which she was riding hung suspended over some river, she would sink deeply into her seat, eyes closed, breath coming through her nostrils in short whistling gusts, moaning softly, holding herself perfectly still with the brimming cup of her fear clutched between her palms as if she dared not spill a drop. As Mr. Panicker drove through Croydon, the swift, haphazard gathering of the city around them appeared to arouse in the old man some allied phobic turbulence. The rasp of breath in the nostrils, the knuckles white as they gripped the hafts of his knees, the stayed cables of his wasted neck standing out—all these Mr. Panicker recognized as the signs of an all but unmasterable dread. Yet as they entered London the old man's eyes, unlike those of Mrs. Panicker when she found herself trapped mid-span, remained wide-staring open. He was, by irremediable nature, a man who *looked at things,* even when, as now, clearly they terrified him.

"You are unwell?"

For a full minute the old man made no reply and merely stared out the side window, watching the streets of South London slide by.

"Twenty-three years," he croaked. "August 14, 1921." He drew a handkerchief from some interior pocket, patted his brow, dabbed at the corners of his mouth. "A Sunday."

Affixing a date and day of the week to his last glimpse of London appeared to a degree to restore the old man's equilibrium.

"I don't know what I . . . silly. One has read so extensively about the damage from bombs and fires. I had prepared myself for a ruin. Indeed I confess to having in some measure *anticipated,* simply out of a kind of, well, let us be charitable and term it a 'scientific curiosity,' you know, the sight of this great city lying in smoking ashes along the Thames. But this is . . ."

The adequate adjective eluded him. They were across the river now, and found themselves caught between and towered over by two high red trams. Rows of staring faces gazing down at them with inquisitorial indifference. Then the trams split off east and west respectively and, as if a pair of water gates had been lifted, the flood of inner London rushed over them. They had bombed it; they had burned it; but they had not killed it, and now it was sending forth growths and tendrils of some strange new life. To Mr. Panicker the thing that chiefly struck him, and had done over the year leading up to 6 June, was the startling American-ness of London: American airmen and sailors, officers, and foot soldiers, American military vehicles in the streets, American films in the cinemas, and an atmosphere of loud, raffish swagger, a smell of hair tonic, a cacophony of sprung vowels that might, as Mr. Panicker was prepared to concede, be entirely the product of his own imagination but which nevertheless animated the city for him in a way that he found at once appalling and irresistible, an air of riotous, brutal good humor, as if the invasion of Europe itself, now proceeding in bloody stages across northern France, were only the inevitable exploding forth of a buildup of jazzy slang and the uncontainable urge to buck and wing.

"That's new," the old man said, over and over, crooking a stiff finger toward some office block or housing estate. "That was not here." And then as they passed the somber hulk, often still festooned with streamers of gray smoke, of yet another bombed-out block of flats, simply, "Good God."

His voice, as they plunged deeper into the changes wrought in London by construction crews and German bombs since that Sunday afternoon in 1921, fell to a harsh, appalled whisper. Mr. Panicker imagined—he had a powerfully sermonizing imagination—that the old man must have been experiencing (rather belatedly, in the vicar's opinion) a kind of foretaste or demonstration of the nature of death itself. After his long absence from the city over which he had once exercised his quiet brand of domination, he had seemed to expect that it, like the world when we depart it, would stop changing, would somehow cease to exist. After us, the Blitz! And now here he was confronted by not simply the continued *existence* of the city but, amid the smoking piles of brick and jagged windowpanes, by the irrepressible, inhuman force of its expansion.

"Ashes," the old man said wonderingly as they passed a huge new area of emergency housing built by Mr. Churchill, like a vast tilled allotment sprouting row upon row of little tin houses. "I had thought to see nothing but smoke and ashes."

They drove along the grimy arches of the Bishopsgate Goodsyard and left the car by Arnold Circus, in a street that was greatly the worse for having borne the brunt of a German SC, beside a neat pile of paving stones salvaged from the blast and still awaiting redeployment. Then they walked around the corner into Club Row. Mr. Panicker was practiced and even authoritative in his offering of a steadying arm to the elderly, but the old man refused his every attempt, having declined even to let the vicar help him out of the cramped interior of the car. As soon as he found himself on the ground, so to speak—as soon as the hunt commenced, as Mr. Panicker could not help putting it, somewhat romantically, to himself—he seemed to shake off the phobic bewilderment of the voyage. He held his chin high and gripped the head of his stick as if very soon he intended to begin swinging it toward the deserving skulls of ruffians. As they turned into Club Row, in fact, Mr. Panicker found himself hard-pressed to keep up with the long crooked scarecrow stride of the old man.

And indeed Club Row had changed very little, if at all, since August 1921 or, indeed, he supposed, since the August of 1901, or 1881. Some long-forgotten business had carried Mr. Panicker here, one Sunday morning years before. He recalled how the street seemed inanely alive with the horrid cheer that haunted zoos and menageries, how the cries of bird sellers, of puppy wallahs and cat peddlers intermingled and created an eerie and disturbing echolalia, at once mocking of and mocked by the chatter of their caged and staring stock in trade. In spite of the fact that he had known perfectly well, as he passed them, that the lorikeets and budgerigars, the spaniels and tabbies, and even the odd sharp-eyed weaselish thing, were to be sold and purchased as pets, Mr. Panicker had not been able to rid himself, as he proceeded along Club Row on that forgotten errand, of the notion that he was walking down a street of the condemned, and that all of this sad caged animal flesh was intended only for the slaughter.

Today, however, the Row was silent, haunted only by the litter and faint invisible gutter-drip of the Monday after market day. Torn wrappers, bits of greasy newsprint, twisted hanks of rag, sawdust caked in puddles of fluids on whose nature Mr. Panicker preferred not to speculate. The stalls and shops dark behind their curtains of articulated bars and padlocked steel shutters. Above the storefronts, the low, disreputable buildings jostled one another, in serried ranks, like rounded-up suspects trying to exhibit a collective and wholly spurious innocence, while their brick cornices leaned ever so slightly inward over the row, as if to peer into the breast pockets of passing marks. It was, or ought to have been, a singularly depressing prospect. And yet the verve and energetic tread of the old man, the vaguely drum-majorish way in which he swung his heavy stick, inspired Mr. Panicker with a giddy and surprising optimism. He felt a mounting sense, as they headed down toward Bethnal Green Road—a sense that had obscure roots in that vanished market morning when he had passed amid the hectic stalls of the dealers in animals—that they were penetrating to the heart of some authentic mystery of London, or perhaps of life itself; that at last, in the company of this singular old gentleman whose command of mystery had at one time been spoken of as far away as Kerala, he might discover some elucidation of the heartbreaking clockwork of the world.

"Here," the old man said, with a sidewise thrust of his stick. Its plated head rang against a small enameled sign, affixed with rusted screws to the brick front of number 122, that read BLACK, and then in smaller type beneath this, BIRDS RARE AND EXOTIC. A grating was drawn across the front but through the murky window Mr. Panicker could make out the vaguely Asiatic shapes of gabled cages and even perhaps the flutter of a wing or tail feather, ghostly as a breeze that stirred the dust. A faint but animated whistling pierced gloom, glass, and shutters, rising and complicating itself as his ears became attuned to it. Doubtless the old man's rapping had roused the denizens of Black's shop.

"Nobody home," Mr. Panicker said, pressing his forehead against the morning-cool steel of the grate. "We ought not to have come on a Monday."

The old man raised his stick and struck the grate, again and again, with gleeful savagery, eyes alight at the clang and the ringing of steel. When he stopped, the shadowy population of the shop had been thrown or had thrown themselves into pandemonium. The old man stood with his stick held high, chest heaving, a fleck of spittle on his cheek. The clamor of the rage resounded and died. The light went from his eyes.

"A Monday," said the old man sadly. "I ought to have foreseen this."

"Perhaps you might have rung in advance," Mr. Panicker said. "Made an appointment with this Black chap."

"No doubt," the old man said. He lowered his stick to the pavement and then, sagging, leaned heavily upon it. "In my haste I . . ." He wiped at his cheek with the back of a hand. "Such practical considerations seem to lie beyond my . . ." He lurched forward, and Mr. Panicker caught his arm, and this time the old man failed to shrug him off. His eyes stared as if blindly at the unanswering face of the shop, his face inhabited only by a hint of elderly alarm.

"There there," Mr. Panicker murmured, seeking to ignore and conceal the brutality of his own disappointment at the sudden failure of their quest. He had begun the day sleepless, drunk, and contemplating the bombed-out house of his life as a man. His vacant marriage, his useless son, the eclipse of his professional ambitions, these were the shattered windows, the scorched wallpaper, and twisted fauteuils of that wreckage; and lying over all of it like a snowfall of ash, hanging in the air like an ineradicable pall of smoke, layer after charred layer reaching all the way down to bedrock, was the knowledge of his own godlessness, of his doubt and unbelief and the distance of his own heart from that of Christ the Lord. A minor Blitz, of no concern to anyone; the falling bomb—like all bombs a chance and mindless thing—the arrival and murder of Mr. Richard Shane. At the moment of impact the whole rotten structure had collapsed and it was as if, as Mr. Panicker had seen described in newspaper accounts of the Blitz, all of the hundreds of rats dwelling in the walls of the edifice were exposed, suspended and surprised in their customary leering attitudes, before their bodies came plopping to earth in a sickening gray shower of rat. And yet, as he had also read, from time to time such explosions had been known to discover the glint of odd and surprising treasure. Rare things, delicate things that, unknown, unobserved, had been there all along. This morning on the London road, when the old man had swept into the car in his mantle of wool and rain, it was as if the boy, Linus Steinman, bereft and friendless, had been thus revealed, standing tiny and alone in the midst of the heap of gray ash, eyes trained longingly on the sky. Mr. Panicker was not so hopeful or so foolish as to imagine that finding a refugee boy's missing parrot would restore the meaning and purpose to his life. But he had been willing to settle for so very much less.

"Perhaps we might return another day. Tomorrow. We could put up in a hotel tonight. There's a very decent little place I know."

Abruptly Mr. Panicker's earlier fantasy of the Crampton Hotel, with its really excellent breakfast, sprung, vividly and temptingly, back to life. Only now, in the place of seminars and presentations that even in fancy could only be imagined as repetitious and interminably dull there was, in the company of this mad old beekeeper, the unlikely possibility, all the more splendid for its unlikeliness, of adventure. The man seemed, in a way that Mr. Panicker would have been hard-pressed to explain or instance, not only to generate or to invite such a possibility but, somehow, implicitly to require a confederate in its undertaking. It was this possibility, even more than the sense of altruistic mission and opportunity for redemption represented by retrieval of a boy's lost bird, that Mr. Panicker now found himself battling to sustain. For what, in the end, had drawn him, a gangly barefoot Malayalee country boy, into the life of a Minister of the Church of England? Naturally it had been a question—and so, to the point of tedium and nonsense, had he incessantly repeated over the past forty years—of one's answering a call. Only now, however, did it occur to him that the call was neither, as he had once supposed, divine or mystical in origin nor, as he had later bitterly concluded, a kind of emotional *ignis fatuus*. How many rude and shoeless young men, he wondered, set off in search of adventure, believing with all their hearts that they were answering a summons from God?

"Come!" Mr. Panicker said. "Wait here. I will fetch the car. We'll take a pair of rooms at the Crampton and arrange to meet this Black—we'll lay a very trap for him!"

The old man nodded, slowly, his expression abstract, his

eyes dull, barely registering the words. In the aftermath of his moment of confusion and alarm a deep melancholy seemed to have come over him. It was in stark contrast to the sense of readiness, of irrepressible fitness to continue the game, that now animated Mr. Panicker. He ran all the way to Boundary Street, leapt into the Imperia, and hurried back to retrieve his co-adventurer. As he neared Black's shop the old man did not move. He stood hunched over, balanced on his stick, in precisely the same way in which Mr. Panicker had left him. Mr. Panicker pulled up alongside the curb and set the hand brake. The old man stood, gazing down at his great boots. After a moment Mr. Panicker sounded the horn, one two. The old man raised his head, slowly, and peered toward the front passenger window of the car as if he had no idea whom he might find within. Just before Mr. Panicker leaned over to roll the window down, however, the old man's face suddenly altered. He arched an eyebrow, and his eyes narrowed slyly, and a long thin smile twisted one of the corners of his mouth.

"No, you fool!" he cried, as Mr. Panicker lowered the window. "Roll it back up!"

Mr. Panicker complied, and as he did so the grin on the old man's face widened and spread very wonderfully, and he said something that Mr. Panicker failed to understand. He studied the window glass for a full minute—he might, it seemed to Mr. Panicker, have been examining his own re-

flection—smiling and saying the mysterious words to himself. Even when, having got into the car alongside Mr. Panicker, he repeated the words aloud, the minister found
himself at a loss.

"Leg ov red!" the old man repeated inanely. "As is ever
the case, ha ha, a matter of *reflection*! Leg ov red!"

"I—I'm sorry, sir. I fail to understand—"

"Quickly! What features characterize the Steinman
boy's scratchings in that notebook of his?"

"Well, he has the strange trait, of course, of reversing
his words. Mirror writing. Apparently, according to the doctors, it's related in some way to his inability to speak. Some
sort of trauma, no doubt. And then I have noticed that he is
an execrable speller."

"Yes! And when, in what I now perceive to have been a
pathetic plea for assistance, he scrawled the words 'leg ov
red' on a bit of paper, he was neatly exhibiting both traits."

"Leg ov red," Mr. Panicker tried, projecting and reversing the letters against an interior screen. "Der . . . Vog . . .
el." Ah. "Der Vogel. He was asking after the bird. Of
course."

"Yes. And now, tell me what he was saying on the *other*
side of the scrap."

"Scrap?"

The old man thrust a bit of writing paper into his hands.

"This scrap. On which was written, by an adult man,

young, with a Continental hand, the address of the very establishment before which we now sit. Dropped, or so I mistakenly concluded, by the proprietor himself."

"Blak," Mr. Panicker read. And then, reverse-projecting it: "Good God."

10

He had seen madmen: the man who smelled of boiled bird-flesh was going mad.

He knew the smell of bird-flesh, for they ate it. They ate anything. The knowledge that the men of his home forests would burn and eat with relish the flesh of his own kind was a stark feature of his ancestral lore. In the first days of his captivity the contemplation of their bloody diet and the likelihood that he was being kept by them against the satiation of some future hunger so troubled and revolted him that he had fallen silent and chewed a bald place in the feathers of his breast. By now he was long accustomed to the horror of their appetites, and he had lost the fear of being eaten; insofar as he had observed them, these men, pale creatures, though they devoured birds in cruel abundance and variety, arbitrarily exempted his kind from slaughter. The bird they ate most often was the kurcze Hahne poulet chicken kip and it was this odor, of a chicken slaughtered and boiled in water with carrots and onions, that, for some reason, the man who was going mad exuded, even though he never appeared to eat anything more than toast and tinned sardines.

In the Dutchman's house, by the harbor, on the island of his hatching, when he still feared the fires and teeth of these terrible apes with their strange, beguiling songs, he had gone, he supposed, slightly mad himself. As he watched the boiled-chicken man, Kalb, stalk back and forth across the room, hour after hour, the pelt of his head disordered, the pelt of his face grown thick, singing softly to himself, the parrot would creep, in unwilling sympathy, from one end to the other of his perch, and feel a certain comfort in so doing, and recall how, in those first fearful months with the Dutchman, he had passed hours making the same short journey, back and forth, silently chewing on his own plumage until he bled.

He had seen madmen. The Dutchman had gone mad, in fact; had killed with the knotted-up bones of his hands the girl who shared his bed, then drunk his own death in a glass of whisky spoilt by the worst-smelling substance that Bruno had yet encountered in his long life among men and their remarkable vocabulary of stenches. Whisky had a stench of its own, but it was one that Bruno during the later time of his tenure with *le Colonel* had learned to appreciate. (It had been ages now since anyone had offered whisky to Bruno. The boy and his family never drank it at all, and though he had often detected its acrid flavor on the breath and clothing of Poor Reggie, he had never actually seen Poor Reggie with a glass or bottle of the stuff in his hand.) *Le Colonel* had his bouts of madness, too, silent, lasting glooms into which he sank so far that his songlessness Bruno experienced as a kind of sorrow, though it was nothing like the sorrow that he felt now, having lost his boy, Linus, who sang in secret, to Bruno alone.

It was one of Linus's old songs, the train song, that was driving Kalb mad, in a way Bruno did not entirely understand but that he appreciated and, it must be admitted, even encouraged. Kalb would come to stand before Bruno on his perch, with a sheet of paper in one hand and a pencil in the other, and beg him to sing the train song, the song of the long rolling cars. The room was filled with sheets of paper that the man had covered with claw marks, marks that Bruno understood to represent, in a manner whose principles he grasped but had never learned to master, the elements, simple and infectious, of the train song. Sometimes when the man left the room they shared, he would return with a small blue bundle of folded paper, which he tore open as if it were food and voided hungrily of its contents. Invariably and to Bruno's bemused annoyance these contents turned out to be yet another sheet of little marks. And then the pleas and threats would begin again.

The man was standing there now, shoeless, shirtless,

with just such a torn blue sheet of claw marks in his hand, muttering. He had come in not long before, breathing heavily from his climb up the steps of the high room, and exuding powerfully his characteristic smell of murdered and boiled bird.

"The routing prefix," he kept saying to himself, bitterly, in the language of the boy and his family. This man could also speak in the language of Poor Reggie and *his* family, and once there had been a visitor—their single visitor—with whom the madman had easily conversed in the language of Wierzbicka, whose memory Bruno would always reverence, because it was Wierzbicka the sad-voiced little tailor who had sold Bruno to the boy's family, in a transfer that Bruno had experienced, without quite knowing it at the time but thereafter retrospectively and certainly since losing Linus, as the sense and fulfillment of his long life's pointless wanderings.

"There *is* no fucking prefix," Kalb said. He lowered the sheet of blue paper and fixed his madman's gaze on Bruno. Bruno set his head to an angle that, among his own kind, would have been understood as an eloquent expression of sardonic intransigence, and waited.

"How about some *letters,* for a change?" the man said. "Don't you know any letters?"

Letters was in fact a concept that he grasped, or at any rate one that he recognized; it was the name of the bright bundles of paper that men ripped open so ravenously and watched so hopelessly with their darting white eyes.

"Alphabet?" Kalb tried. "A-B-C?"

Bruno held his head steady, but his pulse quickened at the sound. He was fond of alphabets; they were intensely pleasurable to sing. He remembered Linus singing his alphabet, in the tiny errant voice of his first vocalizations. The memory was poignant, and the urge to repeat his *ABC* bubbled and rose in Bruno until it nearly overwhelmed him, until his claws ached for the give of the boy's slim shoulder. But he remained silent. The man blinked, breathing steadily, angrily, through his soft pale beak.

"Come on," he said. He bared his teeth. "Please. *Please.*"

The alphabet song swelled and billowed, distending Bruno's breast. As was true of all his kind there was a raw place somewhere, inside him, that singing pressed against in a way that felt very good. If he sang the alphabet song for the man, the rawness would diminish. If he sang the train song, which had lingered far longer and more vividly in his mind than any of the thousand other songs he could sing, for reasons unclear even to him but having to do with sadness, with the sadness of his captivity, of his wanderings, of his finding the boy, of the rolling trains, of the boy's mama and papa and the mad silence that had come over the boy when he was banished from them, then the rawness would be soothed. It was bliss to sing the train song. But the alphabet song would do.

He could just sing a little of it; just the beginning. Surely that could be of no possible value to the man. He shined his staring left eye at Kalb, fighting him as he had been fighting him for weeks.

"There is no fucking prefix," Bruno said.

The man let out a sharp soft whistle of breath, and raised his hand as if to strike the bird. Bruno had been struck before, several times over the years. He had been throttled and shaken and kicked. There were certain songs that provoked such responses in certain people, and one learned to avoid them, or in the case of a very clever bird like Bruno, to choose one's moments. It had been possible to torment *le Colonel*, for example, simply through the judicious repetition, in the presence of his wife, of certain choice remarks of *le Colonel's petite amie* Mlle. Arnaud.

He raised one claw to ward off the blow. He prepared to snatch a moist chunk of flesh from the man's hand. But instead of hitting him the man turned away, and went to lie down on the bed. This was a welcome development; for if the man fell asleep, then Bruno could permit himself to sing the alphabet song, and also the train song, which he sang, of course, in the boy's secret voice, just as the boy had sung it to him, standing in the window at the back of Herr Obergruppenführer's house, overlooking the railroad tracks, watching the endless trains rolling off to the place where the sun came up out of the ground every day, each piece of the train bearing the special claw marks that were the interminable lyrics of the train song. Because Kalb seemed to want so badly to hear the train song, Bruno was careful now only to sing it when the man was asleep, with the instinctive and deliberate perversity that was among the virtues most highly prized by his kind. The sound of the train song, arising in the middle of the night, would jar the man from his slumber, send him scrabbling for his pencil and pad. When at last he was awake, sitting in a circle of light from the lamp with pencil clutched in his fingers, then—of course—Bruno would leave off singing. Night after night, this performance was repeated. Bruno had seen men driven mad, beginning with that Dutchman on the island of Ferdinand Po, in the heat, with the endless humming of the cicadas. He knew how it was done.

The doorbell rang, far below Kalb's cramped room. Bruno heard it, and then, an instant later as always, the man heard it, too. He sat up, his head cocked at an angle that among parrots would have signified mild sexual arousal but that among apes denoted vigilance. Kalb was always alert to the comings and goings of the house, in which seventeen other humans, six of them female, dwelled, in separate quarters, only rarely exchanging their songs. Bruno could hear nine of the other humans now, heard their wireless sets, their coal hissing in the grate, the clack of a pair of knitting needles. And he could hear the voice of Mrs. Dunn, the landlady, far down at the bottom of the stairs. In reply came a male voice that he didn't recognize. Then Bruno heard heavy treads on the stairway, three, no, four men, and Mrs. Dunn as well, but Kalb appeared not to remark this clamor until the climbers were well past the second-storey landing and still coming up.

At last Kalb flew to his feet and ran to press his ear to the door. He listened for a moment, then uttered a dark, harsh syllable much favored by Herr Obergruppenführer when he had lain on Papa's couch, in the office at the back of the house by the railroad tracks, a stench on his boots that was almost as terrible as the smell of the Dutchman's glass of death. Kalb spun from the door and cast his eyes wildly around the room, then turned to Bruno, his arms outspread, as though asking for assistance. But Bruno felt no inclination to help him, for Kalb was not at all a good man. He had taken Bruno from Linus, who needed Bruno and sang to him in a way that deeply repaid all the long years of suffering and captivity; and, what was more, Kalb was a killer of his fellow men—Bruno had seen him strike down the man called Mr. Shane, from behind, with a hammer. It was true, of course, that Mr. Shane had also been planning to take Bruno from Linus; nonetheless Bruno would never have desired his death, and hated the ineradicable memory of having witnessed it.

He determined to inform Kalb that he would not help him, even if somehow he could have done so, even if he understood what danger it was that now approached.

He opened his beak and emitted, in a way that pressed

very satisfyingly on the raw place inside him, a series of low chuckling coughs. This allusion to Kalb's characteristic odor, though the man would have had no way of knowing it, constituted a faithful and exact reproduction of the sound produced by the Blue Minorcans that had scratched in the back garden of *le Colonel*'s house in Biskra, Algeria, in particular of one strapping blue and white lady whose coloration Bruno had always admired.

The next moment he paid rather dearly for his little joke, however, when the man snatched up a canvas laundry sack and dived at Bruno, grasping him unfairly but effectively by the legs. Before Bruno could get hold of Kalb's hand or nose or earlobe with the mighty implement, horn and shears and mouth and hand, that was his sole pride and vanity and treasure in the world, he found himself thrust into darkness.

From within the laundry sack he heard the sound of the man gathering up his scattered sheets of claw marks, and then the creak of the wardrobe door. The darkness around him resounded with an unmistakably wooden vibration and he understood from this that he was going to be put inside the wardrobe. He felt his head strike against something and then there was a flash in his skull, vivid as the breast feathers of that long-since-eaten Blue Minorcan chicken. Next a clatter, as his perch itself tumbled in alongside, jostling him; a soft splash of water from the little tin dish attached to the crossbar. Then another creak as Kalb closed the wardrobe, sealing Bruno up.

Bruno lay perfectly still, paralyzed by darkness and the light that had burst in his skull. When the knock sounded at the door he tried to sing out but found that he could not move his tongue.

"Mr. Kalb?" It was Mrs. Dunn. "The police are here. They want to speak to you."

"Yes, all right."

There was the sound of the tap running, the chiming of the shaving brush against the cup. And then the clatter of the lock on the door.

"Mr. Martin Kalb?"

"That's right. Has something happened?"

There followed a brief murmured exchange of song between the men, one to which Bruno paid little attention. He was badly disoriented, and the effects of the man's brutality toward him lingered, ringing in his cranium. This disturbed him, for it seemed to demand to be echoed, repeated—it called for retribution—and yet violence was as foreign to him as silence itself.

"So you have no idea what could have become then of the boy's parrot?" he heard one of the men saying. He recognized the voice as that of the old, broken-down man with the admirable beak of flesh, who had come flapping out of his lair to frighten the boy and him on that dazzled afternoon along the tracks.

"I'm afraid not. What an insupportable loss."

It grew increasingly difficult to breathe; there was not

enough air in the sack. And then a moment arrived when Bruno felt that he might just stop breathing, give it up, allow all the sad wandering and cruelty of his captivity to come at last to a gentle dark finale. He was prevented in the end from doing so only by the unexpected hope, entirely alien to his nature and temperament, of sinking his talons into the skin of Kalb's throat, of biting off the tip of the hated pale snout.

"And you never met Mr. Richard Shane?"

"Alas, no."

Though the man had cinched it shut, the laundry sack was made from rather thin canvas. Bruno gave his jaws an experimental clack.

"Would you have any objection, sir, to our having a look round your room?"

The material offered little resistance to his efforts; chewing it was not unpleasurable.

"Ordinarily, Inspector, I would have no objection at all, but you catch me at a most inopportune moment. One of my children has fallen gravely ill, I'm afraid, and I'm just on my way now to see to her. Not one of my, ah, *actual* children, of course—perhaps you are aware of my work with the Aid Committee."

Neat as Herr Wierzbicka with his great glinting scissors Bruno chewed a slit in the canvas sack, then a second slit running at right angles to the first. He grasped the loose corner in his bill and gave a sharp yank. There was a soft ripping sound as a flap tore away from the sack. It was an interesting sound—*ksst, ksssst*—and Bruno would have liked to produce it himself, but his mouth was filled with canvas and furthermore the hole was still not large enough. At any rate it was not easy for a parrot to sing when it was in the grip of a dark emotion such as the rage that now suffused him.

"I'm terribly sorry, but I must ask you . . . have you come to arrest me?"

"No, no. Not at all."

Bruno gave another yank on the flap, then poked his head through the hole he had made. There was an alteration in the quality of darkness; he could see a shimmering seam running all the way around the edges of the wardrobe door.

"And I'm not—I can hardly imagine that I would be under suspicion—"

"Not at all. But we *would* like to put a few questions to you."

"Then I really must ask you, for now, to excuse me. I have to make a train for Slough in—oh, my goodness, twenty-five minutes. I would be happy to come down to Scotland Yard and speak to you. Later today, perhaps four or four-thirty. Would that be all right?"

"All right, then," said the one called Inspector, employing tones of regret and doubtfulness. There was the scrape and susurrus of the men's feet and they turned for the door.

Bruno struggled, flapping and scrabbling, to free the remainder of his body from the sack. One of his wings struck the cold shaft of his perch, and having found it he gripped the metal tightly with a talon. Using the shaft as purchase on the darkness he launched himself against the wardrobe door, prepared when it swung open to fly at the throat of the man and expose the red meat within.

This time there was no flash inside his skull; it was his body that struck the door, smacking the breath from his lungs like the back of a massive wooden hand. He lay at the bottom of the wardrobe, failed and trembling and gasping for air. He opened his mouth to sing of his impotence, his anger, his hatred of the man who had taken him away from Linus Steinman. For a long moment nothing emerged from his paralyzed throat. The room beyond the wardrobe door was deeply, almost audibly silent, as if all the creatures there were waiting to hear whatever it was that Bruno might—must—manage to say. In the instant before he lost consciousness he felt, rather than heard, the low gutteral chuckle that bubbled up from him, and the words of the inspector beyond the door.

"Are you keeping a chicken in your wardrobe, then, Mr. Kalb?"

11

The boy watched, unsmiling, his dark blazer neat and pressed, his collar buttoned, his rep necktie, which he looked to have knotted himself, dangling limply in the heat. He might have been awaiting the passage of a funeral. The old man stood on the top of the carriage stairs with the wire cage, hooded, at his feet.

The train swayed slowly toward the end of the platform. Lamentations and irritable bovine sighing from the engine. The inspector stood behind the old man, clearing his throat as if in expectation of making a few modest remarks on this satisfactory occasion. It had been agreed among the three men—Mr. Panicker lingered in the corridor—that it was to the eldest of them that the honor of returning bird to master would fall. The old man supposed that this was only fair; he had not merely permitted but insisted that Inspector Bellows take and receive full credit for the apprehension and arrest of the murderer Martin Kalb. As for the minister's reasons for declining the honor, his role in the adventure of the bird's return, marginal perhaps but true, appeared in the long run to have done little to improve his view of things. He had been gloomy and taciturn the whole way down from London, sitting in the smoking car scattering pipe ash all over his dull layman's clothes. He was coming home, it seemed to the old man, rather with his tail between his legs.

Apart from his wife and the boy, the platform of the country station was, but for the local postmaster and a pair of young women dressed for a day down at Eastbourne, deserted. The vicar's son had chosen not to welcome his father home; according to the inspector, Reggie Panicker had fled Sussex "for good one does hope," though the old man considered that perhaps it would have been more charitable to say that Reggie had gone in search of a place where his shortcomings of character were less well catalogued, where his unfortunate history would not forever be held against him, where he would not be the likeliest suspect for every wrong deed committed in the neighborhood, and, crucially, where a vengeful Fatty Hodges would not be able to track him down.

The train shuddered then fell still. The boy took a step toward the carriage, a step so tentative that the old man saw Mrs. Panicker press a hand against the back of his neck to encourage him.

"You'd think he could manage a smile, at least," Mr.

Panicker said, brushing ash from his shirtfront. "Today of all days. Good God. Lucky to have the bird at all."

"True enough," the old man said. He wondered a little, still, that the parrot, until recently the object of intense regard at the highest levels of government, had been so rapidly and without apparent interest discharged from official custody. Amid the absolute indifference of Colonel Threadneedle's office to the disposition of Bruno, there were hints given out that enemy codes had been changed, rendering inutile whatever secret information Bruno might possess. These hints were proffered with just enough offhand firmness as to leave the old man persuaded that in fact something deeper was afoot. Perhaps, he thought, some better, more reliable means of decipherment had been arrived at than a middle-aged and somewhat perverse polyglot bird. "A smile would not be at all unwelcome." In fact the old man felt a strong desire, nearly an ache, to see the reflection of happiness in the boy's face. The business of detection had for so many years been caught up with questions of remuneration and reward that although he was by now long beyond such concerns he felt, with surprising vigor, that the boy owed him the payment of a smile. But as Linus Steinman approached the train, his eyes on the hooded dome at the old man's feet, his expression did not alter from its habitual blankness, apart, perhaps, from a flicker of anxiety in the eyes, even of doubt. It was a look that the old man recognized, though for an instant he could not recall whence.

But perhaps it was not too different from the doubt that haunted the eyes of the Reverend Mr. K.T. Panicker.

Well, the old man thought. Of course he's worried: he can't *see* his friend.

"Here," he said, brusquely, to the vicar. He lifted the cage, not without difficulty, and handed it to Mr. Panicker. The vicar started to shake his head, but the old man pressed the cage toward him with all the strength in his arms. He gave the vicar a shove, none too gently, toward the stair. Then as Mr. Panicker hesitantly stepped down from the train, the old man reached over with a crooked trembling arm and tugged the oilcloth hood from the cage, revealing with a conjuror's flourish the scarlet tail, the powerful black bill, the bottomless black eyes, the legs of red.

The boy smiled.

Mr. Panicker ruffled his hair, a little stiffly. Then he turned to face his wife.

"Well done, Mr. Panicker," she said, and she offered him her hand.

The boy took the cage from Mr. Panicker, and lowered it to the platform. He worked the wire latch, opened the cage door, and thrust in his hand and arm. Bruno stepped nimbly on, and then as the boy drew him out, inched his way up the dark blue sleeve to the shoulder, where, in an echo conscious or accidental of the vicar's awkward gesture of a moment before, he worked his bill tenderly through the dark curls above the boy's right ear.

Mrs. Panicker watched for a moment, her own smile at the sight of bird and boy reunited both ironic and wistful, as one might contemplate the salt and pepper shakers or favorite pair of socks that alone survived the burning of one's house to the ground. Then she turned to the inspector.

"So is he rich, then?" she said.

"He very well might be," Inspector Bellows said. "But so far as we—or, I might add, as Mr. Kalb—has been able to determine, those endless digits of the bird's do not in fact represent numbered Swiss bank accounts. Even though Kalb had his brother working overtime in Zurich trying to track them down." Mrs. Panicker nodded. She had suspected as much. She went over to stand with her husband, the boy, and Bruno.

"Hello," the parrot said.

"Hello, yourself," she said to the parrot.

"I doubt very much," the old man said, "if we shall ever learn what significance, if any, those numbers may hold."

It was not, heaven knew, a familiar or comfortable admission for the old man to make. The application of creative intelligence to a problem, the finding of a solution at once dogged, elegant, and wild, this had always seemed to him to be the essential business of human beings—the discovery of sense and causality amid the false leads, the noise, the trackless brambles of life. And yet he had always been haunted—had he not?—by the knowledge that there were men, lunatic cryptographers, mad detectives, who squandered their brilliance and

sanity in decoding and interpreting the messages in cloud formations, in the letters of the Bible recombined, in the spots on butterflies' wings. One might, perhaps, conclude from the existence of such men that meaning dwelled solely in the mind of the analyst. That it was the insoluble problems—the false leads and the cold cases—that reflected the true nature of things. That all the apparent significance and pattern had no more intrinsic sense than the chatter of an African gray parrot. One might so conclude; really, he thought, one might.

At that moment the ground rumbled faintly, and in the distance, growing nearer, there was the cry of iron wheels against iron rails. A train was passing through the station, a freight, a military transport, its cars painted dull gray-green, carrying shells and hams and coffins to stock the busy depots of the European war. The boy looked up as it tottered past, slowing but not coming to a stop. He watched the cars, his eyes flicking from left to right as if reading them go by.

"Sieben zwei eins vier drei," the boy whispered, with the slightest hint of a lisp. *"Sieben acht vier vier fünf."*

Then the parrot, startled perhaps by the clamor of the passing train, flew up into the rafters of the station roof, where, in flawless mockery of the voice of a woman whom none of them would ever meet or see again, it began, very sweetly, to sing.